Theta Corps

VINDICATION

ALIYAH BURKE

Vindication
ISBN # 978-1-78686-341-6
©Copyright Aliyah Burke 2017
Cover Art by Posh Gosh ©Copyright December 2017
Interior text design by Claire Siemaszkiewicz
Totally Bound Publishing

Published in 2017 by Totally Bound Publishing, Think Tank, Ruston Way, Lincoln, LN6 7FL, United Kingdom.

Totally Bound Publishing is an imprint of Totally Entwined Group Limited.

Totally Bound Publishing books by Aliyah Burke:

In Aeternum
Casanova in Training
Harbour of Refuge
Protected by Shadows
Polar Opposites

Theta Corps
Restitution
Contrition
Vindication

Interludes
Temporary Home
Alone With You
Till We Ain't Strangers Anymore

Astral Guardians
Chasing the Storm
Highlands at Dawn
Fields of Thunder
Branded by Frost
Driven by Night
Moon of Fire

What's Her Secret?
Preconception

VINDICATION

Dedication

Thank you to all who've asked me for Beau's story.
It was a long time in coming but here he is. Enjoy!
To DH, as always, thank you for being you.

Chapter One

"Darlin', if you let me out of these handcuffs I can show you a *really* good time." Beauregard Lee Jackson flexed his fingers and rotated his stiff wrists, trying to ease the pain leeching through them at the confines of the metal bracelets he wore. "I'm as much a fan of being tied up as the next man but this isn't quite fair."

He sat on the floor, hands behind him securing him to a wall pipe beside an old radiator heater, which thankfully wasn't running.

Movement from the other room grabbed his attention with the swiftness of a rattler giving a warning about encroaching on his territory. So did the noise emanating from the same space. That was nothing more than the sound of a bullet being chambered into a sidearm. All thoughts of play and sex went out of the window in a flash.

The brunette who'd somehow managed to get him in this predicament peeked her head back around the corner, a smile showing off her overbleached, perfect, straight teeth.

She batted her lashes a few times before she shrugged and glanced down to something only she could see behind the wall. He bet the gun she'd just put a round into. *At least it isn't a shotgun.*

"I'll be right with you, lover. Have you figured out where you know me from yet?"

Looneyville didn't seem like a good answer so he merely shook his head.

Seriously, I get it, I must have been drugged. But I'm no small man and ain't no way that little thing carried me up here alone and secured me. She must be working with at least one other person.

Thoughts that didn't make him any happier. He refocused his attention on the woman who continued to watch him and forced a smooth, sexy smile to cross his features. It'd worked before — he had every belief it would once more.

She clucked her tongue at him and waggled a finger. "Keep thinking. You should know me, easy. I'll be ready for you in a moment." A high-pitched giggle, which grated on his taut nerves, escaped her mouth before she vanished from view.

He had a good memory for people he'd met before. However, this one just didn't seem like anyone whose path he'd crossed. But there were those days in college when he didn't do much remembering of anything aside from his drink.

Doesn't matter who she is if her plan is to pump me full of lead and give me lead poisoning. That's not anything I need. Or want. I've still got things to do, women to see and people to kill.

"How about you give me a hint?" he asked, loud enough to cover the sound of him working on loosening the pipe she'd locked him to.

More tittering. She popped back into view. "Well, I can assure you, I didn't look like this."

"I would agree. I wouldn't have forgotten anyone as beautiful as you." The compliment slipped without thought from his tongue. He tossed them out without care or consideration. Always had, it was part of his nature. He was a flirt.

Her eyes narrowed before she disappeared from his line of sight yet again.

"So beauty is all that matters to you?"

"Not at all, but you are gorgeous." The bar keeping him there loosened a tiny bit. "Now, come on. At least give me the state I met you in."

There wasn't any hint of a foreign accent in her tone so he wondered if she was from this country, but then again, he could have an accent on command so perhaps that wasn't the best thought.

"I've even met our Grams."

His blood slowed in his veins, much like being turned to tar. Fury raged within him. This psychotic bitch had him handcuffed, was putting bullets into guns, before she went and mentioned his grandmother, Mrs. Maybelle, as if they were discussing the weather? *Fuck that. Don't fuck with family.* At least not his.

He swallowed and ensured that his voice betrayed not a single shred of the murderous intent within him. "A lot of people know Grams."

However, most called her Mrs. Maybelle if they weren't really close, or preferred to.

"True, but I've been in her house. Recently even. We had coffee and pie the other day. I believe it was a chess pie. I got the first slice. At *her* insistence. She told me she'd not made one in a while. I was glad to have it with her, it was delicious. She's an amazing cook."

Five days ago, Grams had made a fresh chess pie. He knew because he'd been on the phone talking to her and she'd mentioned it cooling.

Still not making sense. I'm not even in Georgia right now. I headed out West here to Albuquerque to take my vacation. He had a friend out there who he shared some mutually beneficial bedroom activities with and he'd come out to see her. She was good for a no-strings-attached hookup. And he didn't want to be tied down with a simpering female who needed more than he cared or was willing to give.

Right, because the one in front of you falls into that category. She wants your blood. He ignored his brain's unwanted commentary.

"I know you didn't want to believe me, but Grams was the one who told me you were planning on coming out here. Or rather were already out here." She glanced back into the room once more. "Are you following a woman? I wouldn't like that much," she said, shaking her head, a furrow appearing on her brow.

So she doesn't know about Candy. "I'm not following a woman. Just taking some time off."

She pursed her lips and disappeared once more. He coughed and worked the pipe again. A few more times and he'd be free. Thank God she'd not thought to hook him to the radiator itself or he wouldn't have gotten free until she'd unlocked him. Given the gun in her hand, that wouldn't have happened until after she shot him.

However, it did let him know who he was dealing with. Whitney Adams. A former girlfriend. One who he'd allowed past his 'one-time' rule and had dated. Big mistake.

A fact only expounded upon because I'm handcuffed to an old pipe at this motel.

She strode back in from the bathroom and sat close to him. Beau picked up on the unease in her body. Not that it made him feel any better given she held a Glock 21 in her hand, complete with a silencer on the barrel. But a jumpy person with a weapon didn't sit well with him, silencer or not, as that wasn't the part that concerned him.

Not a good sign.

She shifted in the chair, crossing and uncrossing her legs, as if she was striving to find a comfortable seat yet was unable to accomplish the search. Whitney swallowed a few times but the determined set in her eyes was his concern.

"And I know where I remember you from," he ventured.

"Where?" True curiosity lined her tone and she leaned forward a slight space, the tremble in her hand stilling.

Her over sweet perfume scent hit him and he blinked to keep any and all tears from his eyes.

Another cough while he readjusted and worked to bring his freedom even closer. "We met in Frankfurt, Germany. You had much lighter hair then compared to how you have it now. Back then it was the color of dark caramel but not black. You had some deep gold highlights in it along with a slight curl. We met at a concert and went back to your place for the night." He leaned closer, his perpetual grin turning up his lips. "You have a small dotted heart right above your pussy. And your name is Whitney Adams."

I did take her to Grams' and introduce them. Shit, I forgot about that.

"You remembered." Her intense gaze softened and pleasure spread over her features.

"Undo the cuffs."

Indecision flared until she shook her head. "I want to, but no, I can't."

"You can't? Sure you can. You have a key. Just unlock me." Invitation dripped from his words. An invitation he had no intention of fulfilling. This was about getting free and nothing more.

"You know you broke my heart when you left me. More to the point, when you told me we were better off as friends."

She tapped the bottom of her shoe on the threadbare carpet. The flash of the red-lacquered sole gave him Louboutin as the maker, but these shoes weren't new, nor were they in great condition.

"That was nearly ten years ago, Whitney."

She gasped and glared at him. "What does time mean when you are missing the man you loved? The one who was your *first!*" She pointed the gun at him, the end wavering as she blinked away tears that pooled and began to drop from her eyes.

First? By God's grace alone he was able to keep that shocked expression from his face. No way in hell he had been her first.

"And I apologize for hurting you. I didn't mean to. I wasn't ready for a long-term commitment."

The tears dried up and a wobbly smile took their place on her face. "So, tell me you are now and we can end this. Pledge yourself to me, me alone, and I can let you go. We can go and get married and start a family." Her gaze softened and a dreamy look spread over her narrow features. "I'll become Mrs. Jackson and we'll have five kids. Three boys and two girls. Live in your big house and have big family dinners every Sunday with the entire family. It will be perfect."

The fuck that's going to happen.

Outside, the thunder cracked and the deluge began. Leave it to the desert to get those flash rainstorms. He used the noise as cover to finish freeing himself from the rusty pipe. Sure, his hands were still locked, but he could move. Which meant he could run and get the fuck out of there.

She glanced to the window and he shifted his legs to get the blood flowing in them once more. No good ever came from trying to escape on legs that wouldn't work from not being on them in a while.

Whitney snapped her gaze back to him and lifted the Glock. "What are you doing?"

"Stretching my legs. You've had me down here for a while now and I'm getting stiff."

A perverse smile turned up the corners of her mouth. "I always liked you stiff." The smile morphed into a frown. She shook her head and swore. "Stop trying to tempt me." Her hands caressed the weapon in her lap.

"How am I tempting you? You're the one who tied me here. How long have I been here anyway?"

"One day. I brought you here, well, with help from the taxi driver. I told him you were drunk and he helped me carry you back. You're a big guy, you know." That wickedness reappeared. "In many areas."

She pushed to her feet and began pacing, scratching her head, chewing on the nails of her left hand while her right remained curled around the Glock. As if it were her shield.

"Why am I locked up, Whitney?"

She swallowed as she refocused on him. "That's easy."

Beau waited but she never said anything else. "Whitney? You were telling me why I'm locked up in here."

She blinked and looked at him as if just coming back and realizing where she was. Her expression showed how lost and confused she was. Then everything sharpened.

"Because I have to teach you a lesson."

The words fell from her lips in a calm and controlled manner. Whatever the uncertainty and unease had been prior, that had vanished. And he knew that whatever shit was on the menu for him was about to go down. She'd hit that plateau of acceptance — nothing mattered anymore. There wasn't any talking herself out of it, or him convincing her to release him. She'd gotten to the point of action.

"What lesson is that? I think keeping me handcuffed to the pipe here for a day is a lesson in itself. What else can I learn?"

Beau gathered his legs beneath him and prepared to move.

"Fair enough question. I guess you deserve an answer." She tapped the gun against her cheek. "Very well. Here is your lesson. It's to teach you that the world isn't your playground. That you don't get to go around doing whatever the hell you want. That there are consequences to how you behave."

"And how is me being here supposed to teach that?" He kept his eyes on her the entire way, watching her for a tell of action.

"It's a short lesson. You learn because I am the teacher."

Her expression went colder than the assassins he knew when they were out on a mission. She raised the gun. A momentary flash of sorrow before it was wiped away.

"I have to kill you."

He lunged out of the way as the first shot rang out. Glass shattered and he swore as he rolled once he hit the ground from jumping out of the window. Bullets peppered the ground around him as she took more shots, pinging off the asphalt and ricocheting somewhere else.

* * * *

Shannon 'Mino' Tumelo tugged the collar of her jacket up to help combat the whipping winds as she walked from the bus stop to her apartment. Squinting her eyes against the stinging and pelting dirt, she swore. A storm was coming. She'd seen the clouds rolling in from the distance while still on the bus. The bad part was the main part of the storm hadn't even arrived yet. This was just the precursor.

"I thought it was a good idea at one time. Now, I'm not so sure. Christ, this hurts."

She should have driven to work but she didn't mind taking public transportation. People-watching was one of her favorite pastimes. Plus, it eliminated her need to have to worry about parking or gas.

Downfall is this weather kicking my face in. At least the rain hasn't hit yet. I should be able to make it inside before it does.

Ducking her head farther, she picked up her pace. She dug for her keys as she hurried and unlocked the front door to the building, slipped in, then jogged up the four flights to her studio apartment.

She fought off a yawn as she closed the door behind her and shrugged out of her jacket. In her mind, she swore there was the sound of dirt falling from her clothing and hitting the floor. Mino cracked her neck as she hung up the jacket instead of tossing it to the back of the love seat.

"Shower, food and sleep."

Thing was, they didn't necessarily need to be in that order. She was wiped, having just gotten off a double shift from work. Add into that her class load and she didn't recall the last time she had experienced being reacquainted with the backs of her eyelids.

That's about to change right now. My bed and I will have us a reintroduction that will last a good eight or ten hours.

Thunder cracked and lightning split the sky seconds before the deluge began.

Yep, I'll suffer through the stinging dirt over that. The flash floods around here were dangerous — all too often on the news was the story of someone being swept away in one. Personally, she had no intention of making that highlight reel.

Toeing off her boots, she looked over to the small kitchen and sighed. "Fuck, I didn't go grocery shopping." Which meant food options would be limited. "Okay, so shower and sleep."

Her body didn't seem to argue with her on that. Sleep was the priority.

She trudged toward the small divider she'd set up to block off her bed from the rest of the area, steps heavier each time as her exhaustion expounded with every tick of that second hand. After coming around the corner, she froze in her tracks. Her heart stopped, before kicking back into gear with erratic beats.

Her legs wobbled as she took in the intruder. "What the hell are you doing here?"

"Mino, darling."

Her toes curled within her socks at that deep southern drawl. Lying on her bed was none other than Beauregard Jackson. A man she'd had the hots for over the years but wasn't even a blip on his radar. *From my body's reaction, I still have the hots for him.* He teased her and flirted with her but never took it further than that. However, he was very liberal with the women he went out with. She'd seen him with every type of woman, aside from her.

No, no bitterness there at all. Not even a tiny bit. What a lie.

"Beau." She crossed her arms and willed herself to stay there.

"I didn't scare you?"

"This isn't the first time you've broken into my place." *Like I'm telling you I just about screamed in fear and wet myself.* She didn't need to be the latest joke around the Jackson table. Or the Theta Corps one.

His intense green eyes skimmed over her figure. She knew it wasn't because he found her attractive. So she waited for whatever he was about to complain about.

"Where's your weapon?"

I knew it. "I don't need one. Apparently, I do need a better security system to keep out certain undesirables."

He didn't even blink at her insinuation. "Your security system is shit. And we taught you better than going around unarmed."

She ground her jaw. Exhaustion chomped at her ass like a pack of rabid dogs. "Let me get this straight, you came all the way out here to yell at me for something you had no idea I was doing? Or not doing as the case may be?"

"I didn't even remember you were out here until Masters told me."

And the knife was kicked farther into her heart. Then it was turned a few times, just to make sure it was in there good and snug.

Aliyah Burke

"Of course not. I'm not worthy of being on the great Beauregard's radar." *Hopefully my voice didn't shake too much during that statement.* "Somehow, I feel you need something now, that's the only reason you would be in my studio apartment. So what is it?"

"Don't be upset, darlin'. We miss you."

She snorted and shook her head. "Right. You miss telling me to fetch your coffee, set up this dinner reservation. Send that ex this bauble or that bouquet of flowers. You used me as much as Masters did and I didn't even work for you."

"Now you sound jealous."

She had been. And obviously lying to herself all this time that she'd gotten over her anger and jealousy. "I'm not having this discussion with you. What do you want? We don't need to catch up. I need to sleep."

"Remember when I showed up at your place before we brought Ethan back?"

Like she could forget that. She still had dreams where that visit took a different turn. Yet another thing she wouldn't be telling him about.

"What about it?"

"I'm shot again. Which is why I'm lying here and not standing."

"Of course, you'd only be in my bed if you couldn't possibly stand on your own. Heaven forbid there would ever be another reason."

His green eyes twinkled in the low light. "See, darlin'? There's more of that jealousy. And while I would love to delve into why you feel the need to be so jealous of me and what I just said, when you know you've always been my girl, I'm still bleeding."

His girl. If only. Shoving that thought far, far away, she added her exhaustion to that little corner. There wasn't any way she could ignore him bleeding there. It wasn't how she did things. She shifted her gaze to where he had his left arm pressed close to his side.

"Could have sank your ass in my bathroom where it would have been easier to clean," she snapped, moving toward him.

"Maybe I wanted to be in your bed."

His words may have created flutters in her belly but she was focused on the blood she could now both see and smell. He'd stuffed some towels beneath him but there was a lot of blood. All over her light-colored towels.

"You need a doctor."

"So stitch me up."

"I can't do it here." She tucked some hair behind her ear. "Plus, I'm not a doctor." *Yet.*

"You've done it before. Do it again."

There went that command in his tone that put her teeth on edge.

"No." *I refuse to get dragged back into his world of lies and danger.*

"No?"

"I'm not your personal punching bag, Beau. You don't get to snap and bark orders at me. I got tired of Masters taking me for granted and left. I left that life." *I left you.*

He struggled to sit and she had to lock her legs to keep from dashing to his side to help. "I need you."

If only he would mean those words how she so often dreamed of them to mean.

"A hospital is just up the street. I'll help you get to a taxi and on your way. Or is this yet another thing that can't be explained to the cops when they come in to see what the hell you've gotten yourself tangled in again?"

"I was shot, more than once, Mino. Where's your compassion?"

"By who?"

Her compassion had been beaten into submission by her pain at how he'd treated her over the years. How little he'd thought of her unless he needed something. For he had always been polite to her and she knew without a doubt he would protect her, but to him, she was more of the pain-in-the-ass little sister when she had been holding a torch the size of which could have dwarfed the Olympic flame for this man.

She'd locked it all away just to survive leaving there and not seeing him anymore. Because the shit of it all was her feelings hadn't changed, and having him here, bleeding or not, was akin to ripping the bandage off, or rather enduring a Brazilian wax. Not comfortable, and it was felt for sure.

"Ex-girlfriend."

"And knowing you, you probably deserved it."

"Not sure why," he said, his voice getting fainter. "I haven't seen her in ten years."

Her concern ratcheted up. She shouldn't be ignoring the man bleeding there. If something happened to him because of her trying to be cold toward him, she'd never forgive herself.

"So what are you doing here in Albuquerque?"

"I was coming to meet a girlfriend. Not girlfriend, girlfriend. She's just a friend who's a girl."

Of course it wouldn't be to come check on me. You haven't done that since I left Theta Corps. But then, why would you? I'm nothing more than a nuisance on most days and your gopher the rest of the time. Her irritation jacked up all over again.

"Then go to her. I can call her and she can come get you." Only this man could be here to visit one woman yet have an encounter with another ex who was upset with him. "Shouldn't be sleeping around with so many women."

He heaved off the bed and she flashed her look to the blood on her blankets. The entire side of his light gray shirt was soaked.

"More of that jealousy."

She rolled her eyes. Beau didn't even know how right it was. But hey, it wasn't as if the guy was a troll or something like that. He wasn't. What he was, was big, muscular and hot as all get-out. He had shoulder-length blond-brown hair, always rakish and messy, as if some woman had just finished running her fingers through it. Knowing him, she probably had. Those damn green eyes that glittered like emeralds could, and did, found everything she tried to hide.

"Mino, are you seriously going to let me bleed to death here?" It took several tries for him to get out of bed.

"Should have gone to the hospital. I don't need to be in your mess of exes trying to kill you."

He wobbled on his feet and she groaned.

"Christ, if you fall over I'll never get you up. You're too damn big."

"Yes, I've heard that before."

She muttered under her breath and moved to his side, assisting him back to the bed. He grunted when he hit the mattress—this man did make her double bed look small. Okay, so maybe she'd let him drop a bit harshly but damn it all, there went her thoughts of a shower and bed. Right now, he was in her bed and even if he wasn't, she couldn't use it until she'd stripped it and remade the damn thing. It was most likely ruined from his bleeding all over it.

He even had his stupid, dirty and oil-stained John Deere cap by her pillow and that made her melt. It wasn't fair. Truly, it wasn't.

When she'd left Theta Corps she'd had difficulty wrapping her head around the fact that she wouldn't see him again. Sure, they argued and fought but damn if he didn't make for a nice vision when he strolled into Masters' office with his unhurried, almost lazy movements. She'd seen him a few times out of work as well and he'd always had some hot chick on his arm. He almost never went out with the same woman twice, so if he was here to visit one, she must be the one for him. And that was yet another nail in the coffin around her heart.

"I'm sure you have, probably, have it taped over your mirror so you see it daily."

"If you came to my house you could see."

"I'm not the type of woman who goes to your house."

He narrowed his eyes. "What's that supposed to mean?"

She shook her head. "You have a choice — we can discuss that or you can lie there quietly while I fix your wounds. I'm not doing both."

"Fix me." He dropped his head back on her pillow with a groan.

"Would that I could," she growled low in her throat.

Even passed out, the man was just too damn sexy for his own good.

Why the hell did you have to come crashing and bleeding back into my life, Beauregard Lee Jackson?

Chapter Two

Beau went from out to alert in the space of a heartbeat. He closed his fingers and hated there wasn't a gun in his hand.

"Don't worry about it, I just took it out of the way when I was working on you. The Bersa is on my kitchen counter."

Mino's voice had him opening his eyes. The room remained almost dark but he could see her sitting in a chair a short distance from him. "You know it's a Bersa?"

"Hard not to work at Theta Corps and pick some things up." She rose and padded close, bringing with her a light scent of clean soap and clothes covered in Starfire images. "How do you feel?"

"Like shit. What time is it?"

"You're welcome," she snapped, eyes narrowing. "Time for you to leave."

He swung his feet to the floor and gazed at the bedding. It was clean. "How the hell did you change all this with me lying on it?"

She shrugged. "Wasn't easy."

She put the back of her hand on his head then his cheeks. He fought the urge to nestle closer to her, tug her against him and fall to the bed to sleep like that. It didn't help when she crouched on her haunches and clicked on a light, staring at his injuries. With her attention on him, he took the opportunity to study her.

He'd missed her. A lot. There were small circles under her eyes and he wanted to take them away. What the hell was she doing to get so tired? Her hair had been tossed up in a ponytail, haphazard and messy, so unlike how she had been at Theta Corps. Hell, some days he wondered if she'd shellacked the bun she'd had to her skull.

Her full lips parted the slightest of distances as she investigated her handiwork. Her skin, blemish free and smooth, was a beautiful shade of brown.

When the fuck did I start thinking of her in this way?

He'd always pushed and picked on her but now, seeing her after all this time apart, he had more feelings right now than when he had set off to see his fuck-buddy friend here in Albuquerque.

What the fuck is wrong with me?

"Do you need me to call you a cab? Uber?"

"Why so anxious to get me out of here? Have a hot date coming over?"

She didn't rise to the bait, sighed, and rubbed the back of her neck. "I'm tired and would like to get some sleep in my bed before my classes start in a few hours."

"So climb in and go to sleep."

She glanced up at him from her crouched position between his legs. Holy fucking shit, he wanted her there sucking his dick while staring up at him with those huge eyes.

"I'm not sleeping in the same bed as you, Beau. I'm willing to call you a cab. That's as far as my goodness and niceties go."

"You're different." He hid his pain and rose, failing to ignore how her eyes snapped to his crotch as he stood before her.

"Life goes on." She pushed to her feet and propped her hands on those curvy hips. After giving him another once-over, she walked away without a look back.

Mino had gained some weight since leaving Theta Corps and he couldn't say anything but compliment it. She'd been too thin there and he got it, she had been run ragged. Not only by Masters but him as well, using her as his own personal secretary.

He trailed her to the small area designated as her kitchen. This place so much smaller than his home in Georgia yet it held more warmth. She had landscape images on her walls and vases of flowers on some of the flat surfaces.

Staring at her ass, he smiled. She did love her comics. He remembered the night he'd broken into her place before and found her sleeping in Wonder Woman pajamas. It was a memory he recalled more often than he'd like to admit. The images on this Starfire one were not bad either. Past her shoulder, he spied his Bersa and reached around her, feeling better once it was in the palm of his hand.

"Which is it?"

He blinked and tried to remember what she'd asked. This woman had a way of making him forget what he was doing.

"Which what is what?"

"Uber or a taxi?"

"Taxi is fine." He hated how she wanted him gone. It wasn't as if he was in any shape to strip her bare and lick her from head to toe. Then again… "Thank you for patching me up."

"Because I had so much choice." She went around the small counter and faced him once the barrier was between them. "I don't work for Theta Corps anymore. I'm not available twenty-four hours a day. Don't ever break in again." She pulled up her phone and pressed some buttons. "Where are you going?"

"Never mind," he said. "I'll call my friend."

Her face contorted into something ugly for the merest fraction of a second. "Of course," she muttered. "The fuck-buddy. Go to her once you're healed up but you couldn't go to her when you were bleeding."

"She's not into medicine."

"I'm sure. Hard to be when you're swinging around a pole and having greasy men shove singles in your G-string."

"Careful, Mino. That jealousy is showing once more." He plucked her phone from her hand and dialed Candy. *Okay, so she even has a bit of a stripper name.*

She glared at him.

"Hello?"

"Candy doll, it's Beau. I need you to come pick me up." He held Mino's gaze.

"I'll be right there. Where are you? I've missed you. And whose phone are you calling from?"

"A friend." He rattled off Mino's address and ended the call. Handing the phone back, he refused to release it immediately. "I'll be back to see you before I go."

"Lucky me," she drolled.

"You could be." He shoved his weapon in the waistband of his pants and headed for the door. "Lock it behind me."

She didn't respond and he gazed over his shoulder to find her staring hungrily at his ass. Hiding his smile, he let it go and continued out of the door. Her mouth may have been saying one thing but she wasn't immune to him and he wanted to discover how into him she was.

Candy roared up a bit later in her cherry-red Mustang convertible. He opened the passenger door and slid across the leather seats.

"New car?" he asked.

"Daddy bought it for me." She leaned over and kissed him, pushing her tongue deep into his mouth.

Beau pulled away. "I'm sorry, Candy, I really need some rest. I got into an accident and just need to get some sleep."

She shrugged and gunned the accelerator, shooting them out of the parking lot with a flurry of spinning wheels.

This was why he loved her. She didn't cling to him and would be happy to date someone else even with him around. They slept together when they both wanted it, end of story.

"So, this friend you were with, is she the one?"

He touched his side and the stitches Mino had put in him. "She the one what? And how did you know it was a she?"

"I called back to find out if I had to come in or if you were meeting me out here. A 'she' kind of friend answered. And don't play stupid with me. She sounds cute. Is she?"

No, cute wasn't a word he would use for her. Sexy. Sensual. Gorgeous. Beautiful and a whole bunch of other words like that. "I suppose so," he lied.

Candy chuckled. "Oh, you've got it bad."

"What are you talking about?" How he could go for some pain meds right about now.

"I know you, Beauregard. Well. I know every inch of your body and I love exploring it. But I also know you. Don't forget that. We've been doing this a long time."

"Is there a point there, Candy?"

"Nope. No point, just wanted to make sure you know that I know you're lying through those perfectly straight teeth of yours."

She slammed on the brakes and he swore as his body jerked back.

"Sorry," she said with a grin. "Didn't want to run the red light."

"You're a pain in my ass."

"I could be. Let me use a strap-on with you and I will be." She gripped his thigh, her fingers moving up to his cock. "Then again, you may just decide you like having a dick in your ass."

"Not in this lifetime, doll." He closed his eyes. He had to get to his things and make a call to Masters.

"You *may* like it," she said.

"Can we drop this? I'm not discussing your desire to fuck me in the ass."

"Fine, fine. I had a new one that just came today. Thought you may want to try it out."

"I'm fine, thanks." He readjusted to take the pressure off his wound. He needed to lie back down and rest.

She roared into her driveway and killed the engine once they made it into the garage. Moving slow, he exited the car and slammed the door behind him. Candy held the door for him and walked him to the bedroom.

"What do you need me to do?" Her question came when he released the sliced shirt and the pieces fell to the floor. "You look like you were shot."

"I was."

She tsked. "The trouble that finds you, Beau. I'm surprised you're still alive."

Some days it was a thought not far from his mind either.

"I need my bag."

She tossed it beside him and he went for his phone. When he glanced at her, she held up her hands and backed off. "Don't need to say anything. This is private. I'll be out there when you're done."

* * * *

Kneading the back of her neck, Mino groaned.

"You okay?"

She peered to her left and spied the man asking. Todd Hastings. A guy in her classes whom she actually enjoyed and hung out with.

"Long night," she said with a smile that didn't have to be forced. She had a blast being around him. "How about you?"

"Same. Want to grab something to eat? I know we're done for the day and I don't have to work tonight."

"I work later so absolutely, I'm up for something to eat."

He dropped an arm around her shoulders and squeezed. "Awesome."

Together they turned and headed to his car. There was a small place off campus that they enjoyed dining at. Ever the gentleman, he held the door for her.

"So, tell me," he said after he climbed in behind the wheel. "What do you think so far of the courses we have?"

"Hard, but I like them." She stretched out her legs and fought a yawn.

"I can take a hint. Discussing school will put you to sleep. What shall we talk about? I know, who are you dating and is the sex good?"

His high falsetto had her bursting out in laughter. "Shut up, you fool. I'm not dating anyone. You know this. I don't have the time."

"There's always time for sex."

"Spoken like a true man."

He flexed his arms then grabbed for the wheel. "So glad you noticed."

"I did and I must say those arms come in so handy when we're doing ambulatory care."

He pulled in to the small diner. The lot was full and people streamed in and out. The sun shone down and she was ready for a nice day. They both left their schoolwork in the car and headed in side by side.

Moments later they were seated at an outside table, with a bowl of chips and dip between them as they waited to place their order.

"Do you have the weekend off?" he asked, reaching for another chip.

"No, I'm on nights."

"Damn, I was hoping you'd come climb Sandia with me."

"I could do an early morning climb if you'd be up for that? Just have to be back in time to take a nap before work."

"Can I nap with you?"

She laughed and leaned back to stretch. Lord, she was exhausted. "Maybe if you're good enough."

"I'm plenty good."

"Of course *you'd* say that. I've never heard a guy say 'I'm horrible in bed' or anything similar."

He shot her a 'duh, no shit' look. "We're not stupid." He pursed his lips as he cocked his head to the side. "However, if I *were* to say I was, which I'm totally not saying, but if I were... Would you offer to teach me to be better? You know, we could practice every chance we got until you could look at me and say with absolute confidence about how good I was in bed."

She almost fell off her chair laughing. "Really? That's the direction you're going to go?"

"Hey, whatever works to get me in the bed." He batted his long lashes at her. "I may need extra tutoring, though."

More cars pulled in. She and Todd stopped joking to place their order. As they continued talking and enjoying the day, a couple approached them. Mino glanced up and smiled at them before turning her attention back to Todd. Glad her phone was on the side away from them, she dug it free and had her thumb hovering over the keyboard, ready to send a text.

She blamed Theta Corps for her nervousness but even now, she suspected the worst in everyone and was overly suspicious. There was something about the black-haired woman that set her on edge.

"Excuse me," the woman said.

"Yes?" Todd put down his glass.

"Just wondering if you could tell me what you think of this place. We've not eaten here before."

Mino ran her gaze over the woman once more and began sending her text. There wasn't any hiding the gun she had strapped to her. Mino had firsthand experience in that. It took a lot to make clothing so it hid the bulge of the weapon without fitting the clothes poorly to the person's body.

Adjusting herself, poising to run and take Todd with her, Mino sent her plea for help.

"This is a great place," Todd said. "We eat here all the time. Good prices and good portions of food."

"Where is he?" the woman demanded.

"Where's who?" Todd asked as he glanced between the newcomer and Mino, who the woman wouldn't stop staring at.

"Don't play coy with me, bitch. I know he came to you."

Mino could only think about the numerous times Beau and the others at Theta had told her to carry her gun. She hated them, so she didn't. She had the permit but didn't use it. There was severe ass-chewing going on in her mind at the moment.

"I'm sorry," she said, determined to keep her voice calm, "I don't know who this *he* is you're talking about." *Although I have a pretty damn good idea. He was in my bed bleeding most recently. And I'm thinking you're the ex-girlfriend he said did the shooting.*

"Beau."

Mino shrugged. "I don't know who you're talking about."

She sneered. "Sure you do. But if that's how you want to play it, fine." She opened her jacket and began shooting. Just sprayed the crowd.

Screams erupted and everyone dove out of the way. Not that she and Todd had a good place to get to. They didn't have any place to escape the bullets tearing into the ground around them, the tables, umbrellas, everything.

Mino cried out as one tore into her. She saw Todd go down and scrambled to get to his side. The woman was there, aiming the barrel of her semi-automatic at her.

"You tell Beau I won't make that mistake of not killing him immediately again. Next time we meet, he's a dead man. And I'm looking for him." The man with her tugged on her.

Mino blinked back tears as she splayed a hand over the bleeding wound on Todd's body. "Who are you?"

"Just tell him Whitney is looking for him. And the only reason I'm not killing you is because you need to tell him for me. But I know who you are too, Mino."

They ran off and raced away in their car.

Mino ignored the pain in her shoulder and looked at the man in her lap. His unique blue-green eyes stared up at the pure blue sky without seeing anything. She gasped and shook him.

Just like they do in movies and it doesn't work then either.

"Todd. Come on, Todd. Wake up."

People milled around her, taking pictures and crying. Sirens wailed, growing louder as they neared.

"Todd," she begged, even though the doctor-to-be in her knew he wouldn't ever respond. Never again would he laugh with her, share some of his jokes, and he'd not be in class. "Oh my God, I'm so sorry. I'm sorry." He had no pulse and there was a hole in his chest where his heart used to be. Another in his head.

She gathered him close and put her face to his, her tears mingling with the blood on his head. The cops arrived and pulled her off him.

She didn't speak, just watched the coroner come in and put him along with two others in individual body bags.

"We need you to come to the station with us."

She fingered his keys she'd plucked from the tabletop. "Fine."

"You can ride with us."

"I need to take his car."

The woman across from her shook her head. "You're not in any condition to drive. We'll have it towed somewhere."

"Home. His mom will want it."

She allowed them to lead her to the back of a squad car. Mino cried on the way to the station. They'd barely made it in the building when a deep, *familiar* voice rang out.

"I'll take her from here."

The voice calmed her yet also angered her in that instant.

The officers with her stopped and she didn't even turn to see Beau approach.

"Who the hell are you?" one asked.

"Beau, DHS."

She didn't have to turn—he walked around so she could see him plain as day. He ran his gaze over her while she did the same to him. How the fuck could he look so good? And in control of his emotions? Hers were ripped wide open. She saw the concern in his eyes but didn't address it. She wasn't able to speak. They were in the midst of playing a role so he could get her out of there and she knew how this went. She pretended not to know him.

"DHS?" the woman beside her asked.

"Department of Homeland Security. She's coming with me."

"She's a witness to a shooting. We need to question her." The woman gripped her arm tighter.

"She's coming with me. Your boss has the orders. We can wait here while you check."

Mino lowered her stare to the tips of her once-white shoes, now covered in blood. The color was a darker rust in some spots while in other places it looked black because there had been so much blood. *Todd's* blood. Somehow it was different from being in the operating room. That was just blood. Now it had a name, a face. History with her.

God, I'm going to be sick.

She followed, numb, when Beau led her to the back and out of the door. A dark SUV waited and he opened the driver's door, sending her over the seat to claim the passenger side.

Nausea churned in her gut as they drove.

"Talk to me, Mino," he said, voice nothing but business. "Are you hurt? You're covered in blood. And what happened?"

"Scratch on the shoulder, nothing important." So it was more than a scratch, but she was alive and Todd was dead, so she wasn't about to complain. Plus, the medic on scene had done a good job of patching her up quickly. More would be required later but it would suffice for the moment. She angled toward him. "Who the fuck is Whitney?"

He slammed on the brakes and she lurched forward, nearly slapping her head against the dash.

"What the fuck did you say?" His voice was low and deadlier than she'd ever thought someone could sound.

That man, right there, was the Beau she never wanted to meet in person. The thick drawl lined with edges sharper than any samurai sword rained over her. Menace radiated off him in pulsing waves.

Yet, she didn't care. Her friend had just been shot in the head in front of her. And there hadn't been anything she could do about it.

"You heard me, so I'll ask again. Who the fuck is Whitney?"

"Why are you asking?"

She smacked him in the upper arm, stinging pain radiating up her arm. He never flinched. "She's the one who did this, who killed Todd."

He whipped them off the street and parked in an alley. Beau faced her, his expression cold as ice. "Start talking."

She stared at him, her own pain of loss surging, fury—*he* brought this to her door, to her life—and she smacked him across the face. As hard as she could.

Crack!

He didn't blink. Nor did he give her the satisfaction of budging an inch. As if she'd been no more than a fly.

Chapter Three

The blow stung like hell but he wasn't addressing that at the moment. He could admit he more than deserved it. At least he could see it from her point of view, in which he was the one to blame for this situation.

Right now, he wanted to know how she knew the name Whitney. Christ, when he had gotten Mino's text, fear had flooded him. He had run flat-out for the nearest police station as he had placed a call to Masters. The requested SUV had been waiting for him and he had raced toward the scene.

His stomach had crashed past his feet to sink into the ground when he'd come upon the destruction. It had been chaos all the way around, people screaming, crying. And no Mino. He'd heard that the coroner had taken three bodies away, two men and a woman.

Praying and begging for this not to be what it seemed, he'd gotten back into the vehicle he was using. He'd been on his way to the morgue when he'd heard they were bringing in a woman named Mino who had been right there, who'd been seen speaking to the man and woman who'd shot up the diner. So, he'd gone to get her with another call from Masters to get some strings pulled.

He hadn't given a damn if he went as FBI or DHS, he'd just needed to get her out of there. Now she mentioned Whitney's name.

However, right here, right now, all he knew was that he'd damn near lost her and he wouldn't have ever forgiven himself if that had happened. He needed her in his life.

Beau undid her belt and yanked her to him, slamming his mouth over hers. His fear, worry and anger all poured from him to her via the kiss. She pounded on his chest and he released her.

"This is your fault," she accused, pain leeching from her words, not commenting on the kiss. Although it wasn't hard to see the shock in her expression or her dilated pupils.

"What are you talking about?" He was trying to focus on something other than how fucking amazing her lips had been beneath his.

"She asked me where you were. Your bitch came there to *me,* looking for *you.* It's your fault Todd is dead."

The hatred in her tone ripped him up in a way no other person on the face of the earth could come close to accomplishing. "Mino, please."

She hopped out and strode farther into the alley. Beau jumped out after her. He gripped her shoulder and stopped her from hitting him again. He saw blood on his hand as he curled it around her wrist and recalled her stating she'd been scratched.

The blood soaking through her shirt was from more than a scratch.

"I think you've hit me already." He did his damnedest to ignore the sight of her blood on his palm. Not easy as it churned his gut. Additional amounts of the red liquid could have been out there. She could have been taken from him today. In a permanent status.

"You deserve so much more," she said, legs giving out on her.

He stopped her from sinking to the nasty ground, adjusting his hold on her to keep her upright along with himself, his own injuries reminding him that he wasn't unscathed, but he ignored that pain.

"I know." So much more, he'd brought this back to her door. Involved her in his mess once more.

"This isn't a joke, Beau. I have to talk to his mother and tell her that her only child is now dead because you had pissed off some ex-girlfriend come looking for you because you fuck everything that moves. And because I, from whatever sense of stupid, misfucking sense of loyalty to you that I should have tossed away the second I walked away from Theta Corps and you, was unable to cut ties with, he got murdered as she made her point she wanted answers. Now she's alone and I lost a good friend." Her chest heaved as she cried.

You'll never lose that loyalty, Mino. Never. And he owed her so much for that, the sacrifice she'd made. He didn't tell her that even had she given up what she'd known about his location—which wasn't anything in truth—Whitney would have shot them both and done what she'd done anyway.

He dipped and scooped her off her feet. Carrying her back to the vehicle, he touched the Bluetooth and placed a call.

"What's going on?" his boss answered immediately.

"Mino's alive, took a bullet. I need to get her fixed up. Whatever small fix there was isn't holding. But it was the same one who tried to kill me earlier. Whitney." His anger grew.

"Where are you going?" Masters questioned. "And do you want them to go with you?"

"No, I'll call Ethan and Anabelle Lee if I need them later. Right now, we're going off the grid. I'm going to get her better then we'll figure out how the fuck this woman knew about Mino. Don't call me – I'll be in contact."

"She's not going to like this."

Beau wasn't positive if Masters was speaking of his wife Anabelle Lee or of Mino. He didn't care. This was his decision.

"Tell her to keep an eye on Grams. The bitch mentioned her when she was about to shoot me. I don't want anything to happen to her."

"On it. Call when you can." Masters was gone.

Beau laid Mino in the back seat and dug to find her a blanket. Then he covered her up. First things first. He had to get some medical supplies to clean her up and see how serious it was. Then they had to locate a different vehicle and go dark.

Right now he had no choice but to head to her apartment. He had to grab some items he knew she would have. Parking a bit away, he scouted the area first and didn't see anything out of the ordinary.

Tugging on his ball cap, he hopped out and locked the door. Making sure his badge was visible, he strode to the building and let himself inside. He called for the elevator and when it came, he popped his head in to push the fourth-floor button. Then he backed out and dashed up the stairs, needing to beat it up there.

Cracking open the fire escape door, he watched as two men waited for the elevator to arrive. Slipping up behind them, he subdued them with a few actions and, after removing their weapons, dragged them back to the stairwell and heaped them there.

At her door, he knocked. "Police, ma'am. We have a few questions regarding the shooting this morning."

The door unlocked and opened slightly. He didn't wait, just kicked it hard, sending it into the person waiting near it, and lunged in. The person behind it was a large man who stumbled into the wall. Beau used that time to eliminate the rest of the people in her studio. Three shots and three kills. Then he secured the man who'd been behind the door.

The melee was over in minutes and he stood over the unconscious man as he reached for his phone. Dialing Masters' private line, he walked through the rest of the studio while waiting for him to answer.

"What?"

"We have a problem," Beau said.

"What's wrong with Mino? Something more serious?"

"No, haven't had that checked out yet. There were four men lying in wait for her back at her studio."

Masters cursed a streak that Beau could only agree with. "Where is she?" he demanded. "Right now, where is she?"

Because of how the man looked upon Mino, Beau didn't get upset at the implication that he couldn't do his damn job and wouldn't have her safe somewhere.

"Right now she's lying in the back of my appropriated government vehicle. I doubt she's going to stay there for long. Her friend was shot and killed in front of her today."

"Fuck. What do you need?" A door clicked and the background music faded. "How is she?"

"Not good, Masters. She's in shock. Like I said, I'm getting her and me out of here, just came for a few of her things. I need you to send a crew here. There are three bodies to dispose of. Correction. There will be four. I need to question this one first."

"I'll have a team there within the hour." A brief pause. "Don't leave her alone for long, Beau. She'll ghost on you."

"There's nowhere she can run that I can't find her." His words were one hundred percent true. He would track her to the ends of the earth if he had to. He clenched a fist and peered out of the window that overlooked the street. He couldn't see his vehicle and couldn't see her. That didn't sit well with him. He needed to go get back to her. "Do me a favor, get me a vehicle to use. Make it clean and not tied to either one of us."

"I'll have it ready. I know how to do this."

He stole a look at the man lying on the floor of the small studio and scowled. Time to get what he could from him and get on his way.

"I'm getting rid of this, will pick up another." He hung up and turned to face the man watching him. "It's time you and I had a chat," he said in a drawn-out way as he approached him.

* * * *

Mino stirred when the door opened but she didn't move. He'd said not to move and, to be frank, she wasn't sure she could. Having worked where she had, she got it, she was in shock and it would, at some point, wear off. She had to allow it to run its course.

"Mino?"

Beau's deep voice added a new layer of warmth to her shaking body. She sat and swallowed while he tossed one of her bags in the back beside her. One she recognized — it had been with her ever since she'd left home. Her tattered backpack.

"What's that doing here?"

"We're leaving." He shut the door and climbed in the driver's seat.

"Bully for us. Why is my bag in here?"

He shut the door, locked all of them, and started the engine. "Because we're not coming back."

It didn't matter that seconds ago she'd watched and heard him lock the doors, she still lunged for it. "No!"

"Stop it, Mino. There were four guys lying in wait for you at your place and I don't think they were there hoping to meet you to share a cup of coffee."

The firmness in his tone froze her. She gripped the back of the seat between them and glared at him in the rearview mirror. "So, what, that's it? Now I have to live my life on the run because you couldn't keep it in your pants? Fuck you, Beau. I'm not going. Let me out of here."

He flicked his gaze to her in the rearview. "This isn't because of me."

She rolled her eyes. "Right, so the mere fact that I've been here, going to school, finishing up my medical degree without *any* issues goes to shit the day after I see you've broken into my place has *nothing* to do with you?"

She leaned forward and punched him in the shoulder. It still sucked he didn't appear bothered by that, but she had pain radiating up and out through her hand.

"They would have found you anyway."

"No one had or has a reason to look for me. I walked *away* from that life and those people. From you. I was making my own way in the world, *away* from the death and destruction Theta Corps delivers." And so far from the unrequited emotions she had for this very man.

"I know you left us."

She scoffed. "There wasn't an us. There was you all and me. The one who did the behind-the-scenes work. Hell, I had to blackmail you for you to take me with you to get Ethan. That's not exactly making me feel like part of any team."

He took his eyes from the road and shook his head. "You ran from us. You left us without a word."

"I was an employee. Nothing more."

"Bullshit."

"Really? What was I then, besides your personal secretary to set up for all your dates, send flowers to the spurned women? What exactly was I? No, I didn't go out in the field as you lot did but I liked to believe I was part of the group. After a while it was obvious I was being hopeful, I'd never be part of your group, so I left."

"We wanted you to come back."

"Really? Because I don't recall seeing you at my place asking me not to quit."

His green gaze locked on to her and her heart skipped a few beats. "Is that what you wanted? Would it have made a difference if I came to your apartment and asked you to stay with Theta Corps?"

Her belly churned and she fought the urge to squirm. Only he could throw her off her game. But she wasn't going to fall for it. Not this time. Flattening her lips, she shrugged. *Yes! That's exactly what I wanted. I wanted to be a blip on your motherfucking radar, to be only for a moment the most important person in your world.*

"I guess we'll never know the truth now, will we?"

He pulled off the road and she took a minute to realize she was at the college and he'd parked right in front of the building.

"Come on," he said, climbing out. "We're going to elucidate to your dean what's going on."

He opened the door for her and she allowed him to help her out.

"We are?"

Beau pulled on his ball cap as he watched her. "I'm not a complete ass, Mino. I know this was a big step for you, going back to medical school. I wouldn't just take you away without allowing you to let them know what was going on." He glanced around. "Let's go."

Yet you would *show back up in my life and throw it into complete upheaval.* She walked beside his coiled presence. To everyone else he may have looked calm but she knew better. He wasn't letting down his guard for one second and, while she understood he was like this with everyone he protected, she couldn't help but get the warm fuzzies knowing it wasn't just for anyone but for her.

Then I should be happy. It's almost like I'm important to him. But I know the truth. I'm a means to an end. And that end goal is Whitney.

He escorted her into the building and waited for her to lead the way. She took him to the dean's office and said, "He's busy. I don't think he's just going to let you walk in and talk to him."

"Sure he will."

They stopped at the secretary's desk.

"Can I help you?" she asked with a practiced smile.

"I'm here to see the dean."

"Do you have an appointment?"

"No." He dug in his pocket. "DHS, I need to see him now."

Mino damn near rolled her eyes. *Of course he would pull that out.*

They were shown in and he explained the situation to the man who held her future in his hands. Once that was squared away, they left and he took them to a police station and dropped off the vehicle.

Standing outside, she shoved her hands in her pocket and rocked back on her heels. "So what happens now? At least I had a bed at my place. I can't camp out here for the rest of my life or until whatever is going on is over."

"We go off the grid."

Her heart stuttered a few times. "Excuse me?"

"You heard me." He stepped closer, the heat from his body surrounding her.

She had to fight the urge to burrow back into him and let him hold her, convince her that things would be okay. Mino didn't know how she was still on her feet. She was cold from the inside out.

"I heard some shit but I'm not sure what you meant to say."

"You know I don't mince words, Mino. I meant exactly what I said. We're going off the grid." He put a hand on her back. "Right now, we're going to have an escort take us to his mother's so you can speak to her, then we vanish."

Todd's mother. *Could I get any colder?* Apparently, she could. For now, she swore she had been submerged in icy water. Buck-ass naked. The icy fingers closed around her lungs, making her struggle five times as hard to draw something so simple as a breath.

Not that Todd will ever be drawing any more.

"Will she be in danger if we go?"

"That's why we're taking a police car and I will have some patrols keep an eye on her as well."

Mino worried her lower lip, unsure about putting her in danger, especially given that she had lost her son today. But she and Todd had been such close friends and she had been with him in the last moments of his life. She owed his mother that much.

"Let's get it over with."

She didn't want to do this. Not at all.

Then, after all that, she was about to be confined in some location with the man who was her unattainable dream. *Seriously, can my day get any worse?*

Chapter Four

Beau stole a glance at the woman beside him sleeping in the passenger seat of the Pathfinder. She'd finally succumbed to the pressure and stress she'd been under all day. Mino had kept it together during the visit to Todd's mother and he'd listened to her lie, convincingly, to the woman about his last words being about his mother. But now that they had switched vehicles and were headed out of the state, she'd crashed. Hard.

She curled up in a ball as much as she could in the seat and was out. He'd taken off his jacket and draped it over her. There were tear stains on her face and he could still see some of the blood on her body, along her hairline.

At a gas station, he'd swung in and picked up some disposable phones then got back on the road. She stirred and while for a moment he debated moving her to the back seat so she could stretch out more, he didn't.

Beau wanted her beside him. Wanted to slice his gaze to the side and find her there.

However, right now he had to get them somewhere to sleep. He pulled in to a small hotel and dug for his wallet. She hadn't moved so he wasn't sure if she had woken up yet or not.

"Mino?"

Nothing. He hopped out and locked the vehicle behind him. Pushing through into the interior, he then waited at the dark-paneled welcome desk for someone to approach. A small woman walked into view. Her brown hair had streaks of white in it. She wore a blue dress and had a kind smile.

"Can I help you?"

"Need a room for the night, ma'am."

"We have a few left." She reached for a form. "Just you?"

"Two adults."

He leaned on the counter and smiled. She blushed and ducked her head before pushing the paper toward him. He filled it out using an alias he'd grabbed from his wallet and pulled out cash.

She didn't pay much attention to the information he wrote down, just focused on taking his money and telling him where the room was on the map.

"Thank you, ma'am." He gave her another smile before grabbing the key and turning around to leave.

He climbed back into the car and drove to their room, parking before the door. The place had a lot of cars but people were minding their own business. He saw a couple who were out walking a small dog, and some children playing out in the open area a bit farther down.

Beau strode inside and checked the room first before coming out and grabbing his bag he'd packed and hers, then turning his attention to the woman sleeping. He didn't even wake her, just scooped her up in his arms and carried her inside. Once she was lying on the lone bed, he went back out to lock up the Pathfinder and get some ice.

After returning to the room, he made his way to the bathroom, stripped out of his shirt and stared at himself in the mirror. A bruise had formed along his side where the man had gotten in a good shot with the brass knuckles he'd been wearing. Beau touched it and winced. Then there was the stitching that Mino had done to sew up his bullet wounds.

"Bastard," he muttered. He stripped the rest of the way and climbed into the shower, hopeful that the hot water would work out his kinks.

He groaned and dipped his head, allowing the streams to pour over him, penetrating the stiffness that existed in him. It had been a while since he'd been that scared and he didn't like it.

Fuck, when she sent me that text, I couldn't move fast enough. Raw fear had pumped through his veins in place of blood. As pissed as she had been with him — for her to reach out like that, she'd known something bad was going down.

I should be happy she called me. He ran the soapy cloth over his muscles, enjoying the heat on him. Scrubbing his chest, he gritted his teeth as he encountered a few other tender places.

He hurried the rest of his shower, not wanting her to wake up without him there. Hell, he still wasn't sure she wouldn't bolt once she woke and realized they had made it to northern Colorado.

Beau killed the water and stepped out, reaching for one of the white towels on the rack. He dried off and shoved back into his jeans. He went to the door as he toweled off his head and peered out.

Mino was still sleeping, or she had her eyes shut. As he got closer to the bed those lashes lifted, exposing her gorgeous eyes to him.

"You have this habit of sauntering into my dreams, Beau. What's the deal?"

He smiled at her words and crouched beside her. "Mino, wake up."

She yawned and scrubbed a hand down her face. "I'm up. What?" She blinked a few more times and sat with a frown as she gazed around. "Where the fuck am I?"

He tossed the towel over his right shoulder and took a seat beside her on the bed. "We're in Colorado, heading north. We're stopping here for the night."

Mino stilled and in slow increments turned her head in his direction. "Ten seconds."

"Excuse me?"

Her gaze narrowed a fraction and he about drew back. He'd seen this look before—it came right before she lit into someone. Namely Masters. The man was scary-looking and for the most part people didn't contradict him. But Mino, she had no problem doing just that, most often when she believed herself to be in the right. Now that warning glare was upon him.

"Ten seconds for you to explain why you took me out of the city. Why we're heading north and why the fuck you're sitting next to me in nothing but a pair of jeans."

"I can't protect you and track down the ones behind this if we're staying in town. I'm in jeans because I just took a shower."

"I didn't ask you to protect me." The words fell from her lips, stilted and daggered. Yet there was no denying her sharp intake of breath when he said he'd just taken a shower.

"You didn't have to. I wasn't about to let you get hurt."

"I am hurt. One of my best friends in the world is dead and didn't we already go over this? How it's on you because you can't keep it in your pants?" Her voice rose.

"This has nothing to do with my fondness for the ladies."

"Is that what you call it?" She snorted and rolled her eyes. "Call it what it is—you're a man-whore. You'll fuck nearly anything that walks so long as she bats her lashes at you and smiles. And, knowing you, she has to be pretty."

"There's that jealousy again, Mino. Why don't you just say you want me?" He leaned in closer and gave her a smile, which most women fell for instantly. What worried him was how much he wanted those words to fall from her lips. He longed for her to tell him she wanted him.

"Regardless on if I wanted you or not, Beau, I'm not stupid. You don't do relationships and I have no desire to be a notch on your bedpost. So while it means I'll have to miss out on the ever-amazing lover you tout to be, I'll be better off in the long run."

Her words cut him. He wasn't sure why, but they did and, damn it all, if possible, made him want her even more. "I'll find this cell and eradicate it."

"Meanwhile, my degree is just having to wait even longer."

"If you're dead, you don't get a degree." He got to his feet, pissed she was more concerned about a fucking piece of paper than her life.

"I would have been fine if you'd stayed away."

Fisting a hand, he stood before her. "Then why did you text me?"

She cocked an eyebrow. "Again, not an idiot here, and when I realized what was happening, I sent for someone I know can handle a situation." A cold sneer lifted her lips. "Figured you'd want to clean up your mess."

Those words hit like a missile that had his trajectory. Words that, had they come from anyone else, he wouldn't have given much more than a passing sardonic grin and nod. However, from this woman, they cut like a jagged blade.

"I always clean up my messes, Mino. I'll get this figured out and you can go back to hiding for the rest of your life."

She shot to her feet. "Hiding? I'm not hiding."

He stalked to her until they were toe to toe. "Bullshit. I completely call bullshit."

"Fuck you. I'm not hiding."

He ran his gaze over her face, about taken to the knees by his need to touch, caress, explore her skin. "You ran from us. From Theta Corps."

"No. I didn't run." She canted her head to the side. "Wait a minute, yes, I did run. I ran far and fast from that place because I wasn't appreciated and I wasn't part of anything. I was just another person for you all to use and push around. All the death, blood and schemes. So yes, when Masters did what he did, I left. That had been your proverbial straw that broke the camel's back. I ran away. As fast as I could. But I'm not hiding. What I'm doing is called living." She ran a hand down her shirt. "I'm living my life, taking what I want and doing something I left in my past."

The passion from her fed his own soul. He loved what he did but there was no denying the scheming. They were a clandestine organization—well, not so much anymore, but they tended to operate in the dark.

"You left medical school before. Why?"

Her smile held no warmth. "You don't have the right to ask me that."

He backed her against the motel room wall and boxed her between him and it. *Damn this woman and the way she gets under my skin.* "What do I have to do in order to have that right? I thought we were friends, Mino."

"A friend would have checked on me when I left work. You never said boo to me. You didn't check to see if I needed anything or was doing okay, so let's not start lying now just to pretend we are friends. I was a means to an end for you. Who you came to when you couldn't get a hold of Masters."

She ducked beneath his arm and walked to the window, then peeked out through the heavy, drawn curtain.

He shoved his fist against the wall and took several deep breaths. He had to discontinue pushing her, had to let her mourn the death of her friend, had to do better, because right now, all he was succeeding in doing was driving her further from him. That was not what he wanted.

I don't know what I want when it comes to this woman. She's always been Mino. Nothing more. But now, after this, after her being in the situation she was in, I can't keep it from my head that there is something simmering between us. A spark, a desire. Something neither of us followed up on.

Were it any other woman he had the slightest thought of fucking, he would become a seducer and get what he wanted. This was Mino. It wasn't right, nor was it fair.

After gritting his teeth, he turned to find her in the same spot where she'd been. By the window.

"Move away from there," he said. Although they were far from where the incident had occurred, he didn't want her visible to the outside world.

She stepped back, releasing the heavy curtain and allowing it to fall back in its folds. "What am I supposed to do?"

"Rest. Heal. Shower. You got shot. We're leaving in a day or two. I have to make a call to Masters and update him on what's going on." He tossed a shirt in her direction, which she caught with ease using her uninjured arm.

Mino gave him her back. Yes, she was being a bitch. She got that. She also didn't give a flying fuck. Her heart had been broken. Todd was dead.

And yes, logically she knew it wasn't Beau's fault. He'd not been the one to pull the trigger, spraying the crowd and taking those three lives, but the woman had come after Mino to get back at him. So, for the moment, Beau would be on the receiving end of her anger.

He did come rescue me, too. I have to thank him for that.

She would. Just not today.

There was no denying the feel of his gaze on her and she tried to avoid shifting beneath the weight of his stare.

It isn't fair. I am stuck in a motel room at some backwater place with the man I've had a crush on for so long yet there's nothing I can do about it. Okay, not true. There's nothing I will do about it.

She couldn't. Leaving him and the rest of the members had been hard, but it had killed her not to see him or hear that deep drawl of his that always curled her toes. The way his unhurried and easygoing speech just did things to her that she never failed to want to explore. With him.

For the first few months she'd convinced herself he was out on missions and that was why she'd never heard from him. But when it had grown apparent that he wasn't coming to say hi or even call to check on her, she'd hardened her heart.

Fat lot of good it did me. The second he shows back up in my life I turn into a pile of marshmallow fluff. I'm here with him now and have to be a bitch because I'm incapable of being indifferent to him.

She wanted to hide from him, lock herself away as she'd done with her heart. But the room held a lone bed or a door to the bathroom. There wasn't any getting away.

He was on the other side of the room, filling the space with his deep voice as he talked to Masters. She turned and glanced at him. Her heart tripled in speed as she stared at his half-naked self.

It's just not fair. Not even a little bit.

The broad shoulders that tapered down to a lean waist, muscles that rippled when he moved, fluid beneath the skin. Faint scarring from his battles and survival. Then she moved down to take note of the way his jeans covered that tight ass.

I'd love to bite that. Put my teeth marks on that firm flesh.

She licked her lips and settled back on the bed. He was right. She shouldn't be looking out of the window. There could be snipers. Hell, who knew. She didn't have the information she used to at her fingertips so couldn't pull up anything. Now she understood a bit more how the client felt.

"That settles it then," he said, facing her.

"That settles what?" *Did I miss something he said?*

"You're now officially a client of Theta Corps."

She narrowed her eyes at his words. "How's that now?" She didn't have the money to afford this group. Maybe if she saved for the rest of her life she would, but right this moment, not even close.

His patented lazy shoulder shrug preceded his reply. "Masters heard everything and said you're now under my protection until we get this bitch."

She blinked slowly, several times. "Masters said."

"Exactly." He offered her the phone. "You can call him if you want."

She leisurely ran her gaze up his form and shook her head. "No. I know how you operate, Beauregard, don't forget that. So you told him you were doing it with or without the backing of Theta Corps and he grudgingly gave in."

He quirked an eyebrow at her. "You don't think Masters gives in on anything, do you?"

She supposed not. "Perhaps that wasn't the right way of putting it, but you, I've seen you work before, Beau. You have a way of bringing him around to see it your way all the while making him think he still has the upper hand."

His smile melted her. "I'm thrilled you think so highly of me, Mino. But this was out of his mouth before I could start. Not saying I wouldn't have used my *considerable wiles* to get him around to my way of thinking, but I didn't have to." He gestured to his body and turned as if he were modeling a dress and some heels.

She bit the inside of her cheek to keep from laughing. Damn him for always putting her at ease and making her forget to be angry.

His green gaze landed back on her face. "That's better. I prefer you smiling and laughing, even if you're trying to pretend you're not, versus this bitch attitude."

That cooled her off. She got to her feet, shirt in hand, and moved around him. With a quick grab for clean underwear from the bag, she continued to the bathroom door, where she paused then went on without a word more to him. The tears began the moment she was behind the closed door. This day had been hell. Her shoulder still throbbed.

Don't complain, she admonished herself. *You're still alive, unlike Todd.* More tears streamed down her face at that thought. She stripped and turned on the shower, needing to warm up. With a glance at her arm, she saw the wound was well protected and she wouldn't have to worry too much about it.

A groan left her throat when she stepped into the stream of water. The heat penetrated the cold shell around her right away and she shook. For about five minutes, she just stood and let the water warm her. Slow and steady, it chipped away at the chill she'd been unable to vanquish since the shooting.

Her arm throbbed where she'd been injured but she didn't care. Right now, this was what she needed. The water mixed with her tears and she began to soap up. It wasn't easy, having been relegated to using only one hand, but she managed. As she stood there and rinsed, she drifted to thoughts of her and Beau. And that kiss he'd given her earlier.

The fanciful side of her wanted to dwell on it and think there was some hidden meaning in there for her from him. But the logical side, the woman who was well acquainted with the man on the other side of the door, brushed it away. He wasn't one to be tamed. Beau loved his wild life and freedom far too much to let one woman settle him down. If and when he ever found her, she was going to be one hell of a special person. And he was never without a woman if he wanted one. They all tended to fall at his feet, driven crazy by the sexy drawl and his hot-as-fire looks.

Even now, knowing what she did about him and how unattainable he was for her, her body still responded. Her nipples grew taut and her pussy prepared for a long cock to fill her. She shook and turned off the water, refusing to give in.

I'm not fingering myself because I want that man out there. I won't do it. I'm not going to succumb to whatever it is he throws over me when I'm around him to make me lose my shit. This isn't any different than if I was still at Theta Corps. He's off limits. At least to me.

That pep talk didn't do much but add to the sexual frustration growing within her. It had been a good long time since she'd been fucked. All her focus had been on school and not wanting anyone else. Even if she'd been fucked yesterday, being in such close proximity to him would have done this to her. He always did.

They all fall short when compared in my eyes to Beau.

Her own fault for holding on to Beau despite knowing he wasn't for her. It was what it was and she couldn't change anything. Everyone had their roles to play in the world. And hers wasn't on the same path as his.

She finished drying off and struggled to get into the shirt. Once she had pulled it over her head she realized he'd given her one of his own shirts. His masculine scent filled her nose and she whimpered, not even trying to hide it this time.

So big the shirt hung past her knees, she didn't want to take it off. The worn cotton gave her more warmth than an electric blanket and she knew the only reason was because it was Beau's.

I'm fucking pathetic.

She put on socks and made sure her panties didn't give much of a line, then opened the door. Beau sat on the foot of the bed, eyes on the door while the television played low in the background.

"Better?" he asked.

"This is your shirt."

He ran his gaze up and down her body, brushing her skin with licks of flame as he did. "So it is. Looks good on you. Do you feel better?"

"Does it matter?"

"Yes."

She ignored him and rubbed her hand over her face. This wasn't easy or fun and she wanted it to be over. However, since she wasn't a 'sit out the adventure' type of girl, she wanted in on the planning. Claiming the lone chair in the room, she scratched her leg.

"What's the plan?"

Beau looked at her before nodding. "We are heading up to Montana where I have a safe house and can use computers and be in better contact with Masters. Then we're going to back-trace this bitch, find out how she got my name and information about Theta Corps and where she hides out. Then I will go stop her and you can get back to your degree."

Not the exact words she wanted to hear, but at least he was including her in the plan.

"When did you get a safe house in Montana?" she asked. "Is that a new one for Theta Corps? Never mind, I know you can't tell me."

"I've always had it since Valentino had his issue. Not one I use, but it's there."

"You're still looking into the Watchers," she said, leaning forward.

He stared at her until she almost gave in to the scrutiny and shifted beneath the weight of his gaze. "How do you think that?"

"Because you said you did this after Valentino's trouble. There was a hint of contact of them having something up there in Montana. And you're all about the revenge and vindication, Beau. So until they're completely stopped, you're not going to let it go."

"How do you think you know me so well?"

"I'm not blind, I see things, and since you lot seemed to look past me as a nonperson I was privy to many things that had you known I was there, you probably wouldn't have discussed in front of me."

A flicker of unease crossed his expression before it vanished. He took off his cap, ran his fingers through his hair then put the hat back on. Shirtless with a ball cap on. Damn it all, it was like every fantasy come to life with him.

"If I looked by you, Mino, I wouldn't have given you my shirt to wear. And I wouldn't be sitting here wishing to hell I could touch you in the way I want."

His voice was low and deep, made for sexual fantasies, and the problem was, it wasn't even him trying to be seductive. That was his natural way of talking. She used to walk around the office so aroused whenever he was there because of what his voice did to her.

His words knocked her for a loop and would have taken her off her feet had she not already been sitting. Belly erupting in butterflies, she gulped and tried to find the words to respond to his statement. She couldn't find a single one.

"Don't ever assume I look past you without seeing you."

She sat there, speechless.

Chapter Five

Beau grunted and tugged harder on his cock as he jacked himself off. He was in the shower, hoping the icy pellets would cool his need for Mino. It wasn't working in the slightest.

With one hand braced against the shower wall, he used just the tips of his fingers to stroke the shaft, prolonging the need. He'd long been past caring about the temperature of the water. His mind was on Mino and she could make him hot as fuck wherever.

He worked his hand faster. Needing more, he curved his fingers around the thickness and tightened his grip. The soap on his hand made it glide easily with the water. Working the palm of his hand along the head, he smeared the pre-cum and shuddered, imagining it was Mino touching him, dropping to her knees before him and taking him into her mouth as she stared up at him with those big brown eyes.

He locked his legs to keep from falling as his balls drew tight. Beau slowed and tugged softer, drawing out his masturbation. It wasn't enough. He increased his speed, rotating his wrist as he worked along his shaft.

A low growl shot from his throat as his cock jumped and released his load, all over the shower wall. Body a bit shaky from the intensity of his orgasm, he adjusted the water to warm and finished washing up. Even after that, his cock still hadn't gone all the way soft but it was better than before.

This woman was going to kill him. She'd been sleeping in the bed — last night after an argument, she'd taken the bed and he'd crashed in the chair that had not been comfortable at all. So he'd gotten up early and jumped in the shower. Now he'd jacked off and dried off. Wrapping the towel around his waist, he shook his head then cracked open the door. The room was still dark and the sun had yet to rise.

I want to get out of here before it does.

Two steps into the room and he froze. Mino was making small mewls in her sleep. Waiting for his eyes to adjust to the low light, he prowled closer to the bed and stood over her, making sure it wasn't her arm that was bothering her. Barely any light came through from the bathroom as he'd closed the door, not wanting to wake her yet. So he didn't have much to go with.

But the room wasn't that big and he reached the bed easily. She lay on her back, injured arm out of the bedding as it had been when she fell asleep. But the one underneath the pile of blankets.

Holy fuck, she's doing what I was in the shower.

There wasn't any denying the motion beneath the blanket. She shifted and he found himself praying the blankets came off. They didn't but he was okay with it. It took the will of God for him not to join her there.

Stepping back, he stood in the shadow and watched her, listened to her moans, her faint cries and her whispered begs. Moments later, she bucked hard against the bed and arched her back.

Fuck me.

She gave a deep sigh and turned to burrow deeper into the blankets. He was backing away farther, toward his pants, when his name fell from her lips.

Had he mentioned he was in trouble with her? Because there wasn't any doubt.

Beau took his clothes and shut himself in the bathroom, his cock again hard and throbbing. He put on his jeans and buttoned them, dick still protesting the restraint. He shoved into his heavy boots and laced them. Once he was dressed—he didn't trust himself even the slightest bit undressed around her right now—he opened the door, allowing the light to spill into the room.

"Mino," he said, remaining by the bathroom door.

She stirred and sat up. "What?"

God, her husky sleep-laden voice just added another layer of steel over his cock, which he didn't need at the moment.

"We need to go."

"Is it even light out?" she grumbled.

"No."

She stretched and drew his shirt tight along her breasts. Another fantasy he didn't need to have at this particular moment.

Mino climbed from the bed and yawned. "I need some pants."

No, you need to lose what little clothing you have and I need to be buried balls deep inside that sweet, tight pussy of yours.

"Bag is on the chair."

She shot him a curious glance but moved to get what she needed. Her movement on the left side was a bit stiff and he sighed.

"Arm doing okay this morning?"

"I'm fine. Just need to check it before we go."

He believed she would offer up that response even if blood was oozing from the wound. She didn't complain, that was for sure. He remembered back to when she'd been with them heading into South America to rescue Ethan. She wasn't a field operative. She had been a secretary but she'd never once complained or slowed them down. She'd held her own and earned even more of his respect.

She grabbed a pair of her workout pants and a new shirt before striding toward him. Since he blocked the way into the bathroom, she paused and arched an eyebrow at him.

"You want to go, you need to let me get in there."

He shifted to the side and didn't watch her go in or shut the door. But alone, he muttered a bunch of words Grams would whip him for saying. He turned on the light in the room and packed up the rest of their items. He zipped the bag shut when she reappeared.

Black workout pants with hot pink designs on her hips and upper thighs—it looked like a tree with branches spreading out everywhere. She also had on a royal-blue shirt with a hot-pink star along the right side. Adorable and sexy as fuck all at the same time. *This isn't fair.*

"Ready." She had his shirt folded in her hand.

He unzipped the bag and tucked it in there before closing it. "Let me go first then I'll come back for you."

He waited for the argument but she didn't have any verbal response, just nodded. While he was glad she wasn't fighting him, part of him missed what would have been the ensuing confrontation between them.

They drove for the day, keeping to themselves. She dozed a few times in the car but never once even offered to drive. Good, since he would have said no, but an offer would have been fine. *I can't have it both ways. I have to get a fucking grip.*

Darkness had fallen when they arrived at his safe house. He pulled the stolen car into the garage and closed the door behind them.

She got out when he did and trailed him inside the two-bedroom building. In the kitchen, she gazed around and nodded. "Nice."

"Thank you. Take your pick of the rooms, it doesn't matter to me. I'll get something going food-wise and get in touch with Masters. Unless you want to cook."

She snorted and shook her head. "I don't cook. I mean, I could boil some water if you wanted me to, but I don't cook and I don't bake." She exited the kitchen only to turn back and smile. "Does this make you my bitch?" Then she was gone.

He chuckled all the while he pulled out a secure phone that was in the house and dialed Masters.

"How are you and how is Mino?" he asked on the first ring.

"She's recovering and we're fine. Made it to Montana."

"What exactly are you going to do there and why didn't you tell us about this place?"

He opened the pantry and pulled out some canned items to whip up a meal. "I don't tell you everything, Masters. Despite your belief we should give you everything. And I'm here because I can do what I need to while keeping her safe."

"Is she coming back?"

He coughed to cover his bark of laughter. That was an entire can of venomous snakes he wasn't about to touch with any length of pole.

"I'm not asking her back to Theta Corps for you, Masters. That's something you'll have to do on your own." He put the cans on the counter and dug for a casserole pan. "I can give her the phone if you'd like to talk to her."

"Yes."

Okay, he'd not expected that but turned and walked toward the two bedrooms. He found her in the smaller of the two, seated on the edge of the bed, looking at her wound.

"Masters would like a word with you."

She reached for the phone and he handed it over. The moment she said hello, Beau walked out. It wasn't his conversation to overhear.

Back in the kitchen, which also served as his workspace, he put together a dump chicken casserole and turned on the oven, waiting for it to heat. While he waited, he unlocked a drawer and withdrew a laptop. He plugged it in and he fired the thing up.

With the push of a few buttons, he activated the security tech his cousin had put in place. Then he began to pull up everything he could find on Whitney Adams.

"Here you go."

Mino placed the phone beside him and he glanced away from the screen to stare at her.

"You okay?"

"Sure," she said quietly. "I just want this to be over as soon as possible."

He understood that even though the words hurt, because it was her wanting to get away from him as quick as she could.

Beau pushed on the keyboard, willing it to bring him more information. It didn't. Whitney Adams by all accounts led the most boring life. At least this one did. He had a bunch more to go through.

Mino sagged to the chair beside him. "Thank you for saving me. I know I've been a real bitch but I do appreciate it."

"I couldn't let you die, Mino. Not ready to let you go."

He cut his gaze to her and watched her roll her eyes. "You don't have to let me go or not, Beauregard Jackson. I'm not one of your women. But thanks for saving me regardless."

He flashed a grin and got up from the table. "Give it time."

I can't win with him for anything.

It shouldn't have surprised Mino, for that was how he was — extremely laid back, cracking jokes, and having an all-around good time. But she'd also seen him in action and understood why people underestimated him. They took a look at him and figured he was some dumb, slow-witted country hick. That wasn't the case at all. But he never attempted to correct the misconception. He let people think what they wanted to.

She glanced at the screen and frowned when she saw the woman there who'd killed Todd. *Beau did say he was going to find her.*

Turning the laptop toward her, Mino clicked on several social media sites, which was where people tended to lose their shit and be dumb. If there was anything posted on her that she would ever come to regret, it would be there.

"What are you doing?" he asked from where he was sliding the food in the oven.

"Checking to see what she posts on her social media pages." Her fingers flew on the keyboard. "Figure out where she posts most of her things from and work back. Nail this bitch down."

He leaned over her shoulder and she took a deep breath of his masculine scent. She picked up on sandalwood and pine but other than that, it was just Beau. Nipping the inside of her lower lip to keep from whimpering, she fought the urge to rub her cheek against his shirt.

Or chest. Either one. In fact, both work. Don't want to be picky now.

"Nice." He touched her shoulder. "What can I do?"

"You're doing it. Cooking. I told you I don't do that." She looked at the places where she'd marked things. "She's doing a lot from here in Montana." Mino shook her head and angled it so she could see the man hovering over her.

If I was smart, I would make him move away. Since I want him there so I can continue to sniff him, I guess that makes me the dumbest bitch on the planet.

"Do you remember when you were after the Watchers and Mansfield was presumed dead until the DNA came back on him?"

His entire body snapped to a rigidity she knew couldn't be comfortable.

"I recall."

"Okay, well, we located some information that pointed to this state for them. Then when you all were hunting for Ethan and got in touch with Bailey she mentioned her contacts had given her Montana as well. But when we located him, rather you did, in Venezuela, I think we let it drop."

He moved to the seat beside her, once again relaxed. It was all a deception, however. "You think there's more to this."

"I'm not the conspiracy buff, but this is the third time Montana's been mentioned. And I for one don't believe in coincidences."

"Me either."

Beau crossed his arms and she found it hard not to stare at his impressive biceps. He cracked his neck and she snapped her gaze back to the screen when he looked at her.

"Can you put together where all these are on a map for me?"

"Sure, give me a few. Oh, no, I can't. I don't have access to Theta Corps' information anymore."

"You're using my login. You have all the access you need. Possibly more."

She didn't make him ask again and just got to work, pulling up notes she'd entered from talking to the trio during their debrief. She had been the one to enter it all in. She knew more about the group than they thought she did.

Once the spots were on the map, she put it up in front of him. "Here you go."

"Pretty centralized area."

"Agreed." She pressed a button and it put the dates up beside them. "Whitney's is the most recent but then I don't have access to Bailey's contact so I'm not sure if they've seen or heard anything lately."

"I can get in touch with her."

She held her gaze riveted to the screen despite feeling his stare upon her face. But he didn't move and eventually she shrugged. "What?"

"Why aren't you looking at me?"

Fuck, that voice of his was like the most damning of seductions, but she knew how hurt she'd be if she gave in.

"Why should I? We're working on the computer."

He shifted his leg, brushing it against her. "Tell me something, Mino."

Her body swayed toward the temptation that was Beau and she had a hard time righting herself. "What's that?"

"At night, do you play with yourself? Do you allow yourself to unwind and experience pleasure?"

It shouldn't bother her. He had always been like this. Always pushing. Doing what he could to get a rise out of her. But then, she'd had an office to retreat behind. Now, she didn't. She was with him in a small cabin.

Her heart kicked into high gear and her palms grew sweaty. *Best way to match this is give as good as I get. If I back down now, who knows?*

With a small exhale, she angled not just her head but her entire body in his direction. Lower lip captured firmly in her teeth, she took her time to drag her gaze up and down his hard form.

Ignoring the sharp bite of pain she got from using her arm to move the laptop, she leaned closer to him.

"Of course. I mean, nothing beats having your lover play with you, but I'm always happy to do it myself." She lowered her eyelids. "What about you, Beau? Do you slip a hand down your boxers and grip your thick cock? Or do you wait until you're in the shower and slowly stroke yourself, allowing it to grow longer and thicker?"

His pupils dilated.

"Do you stroke it? I know it's big and thick. Up and down. Tightening your grip as you jerk, aching for, yet longing to prolong, the pleasure you know is waiting for you once you stop making yourself wait."

His nostrils flared.

Her pussy clenched and she almost squirmed on the seat. "Do you close your eyes and wish you had a hot pussy there to sink it into, or do you envision someone on their knees before you, submitting to you as you thrust deep down their throat, making them take it all? Watching the joy in her eyes as you pump."

The green of his eyes grew dark and stormy.

"Mino."

Her name was a warning. A single word rumbled but drenched in caution. If she progressed down this road, he wasn't going to be responsible for his actions.

So despite the nipples drawn to tight tips, the wet pussy and throbbing clit, she shrugged as if they'd been discussing what to have for dinner. "Sure I do. Everyone masturbates. It's not that uncommon."

Mino turned back to the computer and put her fingers—however shaky—on the keys and began typing in some random information for the computer to readjust the circle of spots they'd discovered.

The silence between them was strained with tension until he grunted.

"You're good, Mino. We didn't give you enough credit, but damn, you're fucking brilliant."

"I learned from all of you. Can we get back to this now and not if I masturbate at night or not?"

The look he leveled in her direction didn't do anything to cool her off. He might have been providing a truce for the moment but she wasn't fooled. It wasn't over, not by a long shot.

* * * *

Whitney gasped as she cleared the water and glanced about the room. Quiet. She was alone. Or someone wanted to make her think so. Keeping her head above water, she pushed through to the edge of the Olympic-sized pool and hefted herself out with ease.

The shiver snaking down her spine wasn't helped by the prickling of her scalp. Something was off and if she wasn't careful, she would be dead. With as much nonchalance as possible, she bent for her towel and lifted it to her face, the sidearm that had been under it now resting comfortably in her palm, easing her tension.

She rubbed the cotton over her throat and took another look around, her heart speeding up when she saw the man standing there, watching her.

"Can I help you?"

"He sent me to retrieve you."

The intruding male didn't seem to give a damn that she was wearing a tiny swimsuit or was dripping wet. He stood unblinking, hands gathered before him, as if he didn't have a care in the world. She had a beautiful body and most men would be lusting after her. Not this one. As far as she knew he was a fucking eunuch.

He wasn't anyone she liked to see on a good day. This wasn't a good day for her. She hated failure. Losing Beau like that a second time had put her in a foul mood.

"Fine." She tossed the towel over her shoulder and gestured with her SIG. "Lead the way." Despite her own behavior, she knew *he* hated to be kept waiting and would rather her there in a wet suit than making him twiddle his thumbs while she dried and changed.

"After you."

Whitney paused by the man who had to outweigh her by a good hundred pounds. "I don't know where he is. You should lead."

He walked out then held the door for her.

Each step filled her with a bit more dread. She could be about to breathe her last. He led her down the long corridor until they reached an elevator bay. Once inside the car, he entered a code and pressed two more buttons. They headed down. She schooled her features not to give anything away.

This time when the door opened, he gestured her to exit.

"Still don't know where to go." This was an underground level she'd not been aware of.

"He is waiting just ahead."

Flexing her grip on the SIG, Whitney stepped out and progressed forward until she found the man who'd summoned her. Correction, men. She was more than a bit surprised to find identical twins sitting there at a long marble-topped table.

Never knew Mansfield had a twin. Hell, for all she knew, she'd interacted with them both. She knew he'd had a look-alike at one point he used during certain events, but that man had been killed when there'd been a confrontation in West Virginia with the man he hated, Valentino Cassano.

"Whitney," Twin One on the left said. "Looks like we have a problem with you and Beauregard."

"Or, rather, you have a problem with him. We have a problem with you not bringing him in to us." Twin Two gave his opinion.

Which meant they had a problem with her and she, now, with them. The fact that the gorilla who'd escorted her down here hadn't taken her weapon from her meant they weren't planning on killing her now, or they didn't care if she tried to fight her way out when they allowed the death sentence to pass.

Chapter Six

How is it that an ass can be so tempting to me? Beau had stopped trying not to stare at Mino while she worked in the kitchen. She didn't have any problem doing dishes, she'd said, as long as he continued cooking. He enjoyed cooking, so he agreed. Now he got to sit here and watch her ass jiggle in the cotton pants she wore as she bopped and danced to the music playing in her earbuds.

Then again, I don't think my cock has softened since she teased me about masturbation. Fuck him, that had been hot and he'd used it in his dreams. In the shower. And even in the woods when he'd had to leave the cabin before he did something stupid like take Mino to bed.

The way she moves those hips of hers, Christ. I'm going to have blue balls for the rest of my life. Or until he got to taste her.

They'd been at the small house for three days. He'd since gotten rid of the stolen car, gone grocery shopping and had multiple fantasies about Mino.

Not so productive on my end.

She had been quiet unless he engaged her directly. Yet when he did, she didn't hold back with her answers or responses. She'd been much more able to give a vivid recollection on what had happened at the restaurant where her friend Todd had been killed. And Ethan was hacking some footage to see if he could pull a name from the man with Whitney. So far, though, no luck. Same with her getting him from the taxi into that motel she'd held him at. They couldn't find any footage there either.

He swiped a pillow off the sofa and whipped it at her, hitting her in the back of the legs. She spun around, eyes wide.

"What?" she asked, yanking out one earbud.

"I'm going to head to town. Want to come with me?"

"Yes." Her entire face brightened up.

While it wasn't all that far to the larger town, he'd told her she had to have him with her to go.

"Get ready."

"I've got like two dishes left."

He rolled his eyes and went to his room. Strapping on his sidearms and knives, he checked his reflection to ensure they couldn't be seen from a casual look. He reached for his jacket and shrugged into it. Heading back to the living room, he paused in surprise to see her waiting by the door. He'd not heard her go to her room.

Whether that was good or bad, he wasn't sure.

"What are we going for?" she asked as they walked out together.

"Thought we could take in lunch there and just walk around."

She glanced at him but didn't argue. Hopping into the car, she waited for him and soon they were on their way to the downtown area. The day was cooler than usual and she shivered as they exited the car.

"Need to get a jacket?"

"No." She shoved her hands in her pockets. "I'll be fine."

Tempted to give her his, he knew she'd refuse and so just got them headed toward a small shop on the main drag. The city wasn't huge, like Atlanta size, but it wasn't just an unincorporated area either where everyone knows everyone's business and who's a regular or a visitor. It was a good-sized city, one of the reasons he'd chosen to have his safe house near it.

He had another reason for having her out. Beau wanted it known this was where he was and figured there was a better chance if they were both out. He was cautious, keeping an eye on the street as well as the patrons of whatever building they were in. He was carrying two bags of things she'd purchased when they headed into the eatery.

Clouds moved in and he figured there would be rain within the hour. They took a booth in the rear and he had his back to the wall where he could see the rest of the establishment.

"Have I been good enough bait?" she asked once they'd been given their menus.

"What are you talking about?"

"Don't treat me like a fool, Beau. I know exactly what you're doing. You want her drawn out. How do you even know she's here?"

"I don't, but this is one of the places she took pictures from."

Mino nodded. "I know."

"Sorry I didn't tell you."

"Don't start apologizing, Beau. It's not you. Don't be something you're not."

He didn't like that statement from her. *What the fuck does that mean?* They placed their order and when they were alone again, he asked, "What am I?"

"Straightforward and unapologetic."

"So I shouldn't tell you I'm sorry I am using you as bait?"

"Would you tell anyone else?"

Hell no.

She pointed as she reached for her water. "There you go then. If I'm now a client, then you have to treat me as one."

He shook his head. "Not happening."

"Why not?"

Does she seriously not see this? "Because you're not *just* a client, Mino."

"What am I then? I'm not your girlfriend, fiancée, I'm not anything with any romantic ties to you. I'm barely a friend. So tell me, why am I not just a client and who exactly am I?"

He wanted to toss her against the wall and show her exactly who she was to him. The object of his dreams. Inhaling deeply, he latched on to the soft scent surrounding her.

"We are friends. And if you're complaining about not being the girlfriend or fiancée, we can work on those." The moment the words left his lips he knew they had more than a sliver of truth to them.

"I never said we weren't friends. I said barely."

"How can you say that, Mino?" He wished to know because it baffled him.

"Because it's the truth."

"Wrong. You know me more than any of the women I've been with."

"Lucky me," she stated with very dry wit. "I'm in the 'friend' category."

"You have been to my house."

"Whitney's been to Grams'."

He narrowed his eyes. "So have you."

"But *you* invited *her*. Personally. I went because we were *all* invited. You didn't invite me there to have pie with your Grams."

"To be fair, I didn't invite her to do that either this time."

"Point is, you have in the past."

She gave the waitress a small smile of thanks when her open-faced roast beef sandwich with gravy, mashed potatoes and broccoli arrived. He loved that she didn't mind eating in front of him and ordered more than just a side salad.

"I have, not going to lie about that. But you still know more about me. Aside from my cousins, you know the most about me."

"Bully for me."

"Don't you get it, Mino? If I didn't consider you a friend you'd know shit about me."

"I do know shit about you."

"Not true. You know my favorites. Color, music, vehicle, thing to do on a day off, even my weaknesses, all of that."

"I didn't think you had any weaknesses."

He shook his head and took a drink. "No, Mino. You don't get to play this off. Do you or don't you know those things about me?" Damn her for trying to ignore what had been blatant between them since he'd met her and her spitfire ways.

She nodded grudgingly. "I do." She took a large bite of her potatoes and he swore her eyes flitted with something damn near to passion.

"Tell me."

His groin turned painful when she drew the fork from her mouth, allowing him to watch her twine her tongue around the prongs. It wasn't flirtatious on her end, she just loved her potatoes, and he knew this. Didn't change his own reaction to it, though. Blood coursed through him to make a stop in his cock.

"Fine. Your favorite color is blue, a dark blue. You love country but aren't above listening to some good techno. Vehicle, anything made in the US is best but your favorite is the Dodge Ram 2500. On your days off you are usually able to be found tinkering under the hood of some old vehicle you picked up at an auction or some farm equipment. You prefer to wear jeans and T-shirts to anything else and that John Deere cap is your favorite."

"Exactly. You know me."

Her expression sobered. "No. I don't. I know what I had to do in my time as Masters' secretary when you showed up with your requests. I know about the color because Anabelle Lee wanted something for you five years ago for your birthday. The vehicle because you're not exactly quiet on what type you want to drive. The auction because there were many times you had me do the online bidding for you while you were on a mission. The John Deere cap is obvious, as is your choice of clothing."

She waved him off and dug back into her food. Beau cut into his steak and frowned. Was that truly how she saw it? Because he had heard all of that and had come to an absolute different conclusion.

"What's my weakness?" He took a swig of beer.

Her smile was sad. "That's the thing—you, Beauregard Lee Jackson, don't have one." She drank her Mountain Dew.

Beau was at a loss for words. How did she not see his weakness? It was her. He let it go because even if he came clean on it right now, she wouldn't believe him. Hell, he wasn't so sure he understood it at this moment. It was the truth that had just been exposed to him, like a shaft of sunlight shining down on the facts laid out before him. Ones he'd kept in the gray shadows so he didn't have to face them. It wasn't a choice anymore, he knew, and he had to go from there.

They finished their meal and he paid. On the way to the door, he saw a guy who was watching him a bit too carefully and his body kicked into protective mode. He wanted nothing more than to have her duck her head while he ran her to safety, but he couldn't.

I hate using her as bait. She should be locked up somewhere so that no one can harm her.

According to her, he had done his fair share of harm to her and he hated that revelation as well. She stood beside him right outside the building and he glanced down at the top of her head.

I can't imagine my life without her in it. He'd hated it when she'd left Theta but had believed she would be back. Now that he knew she wasn't returning he didn't want them to have more distance between them. Quite the opposite—he wanted to close it.

"Where to now?"

She glanced up at him and gave him a smile that warmed him from the inside out. Her vixen, minx and trouble smile.

"Something you have in mind?" He fisted his hand to keep from brushing some of her hair away from her face.

"Thought I'd go find some toys for the night."

Fuck! That mental image of her lying there on her bed, plunging a vibrator into her pussy while tugging on one breast, was something he was desperate to see for real.

He lowered his head by her ear. "You need something between your legs, Mino, I'm right here."

She gave him a patronizing smile. "No thanks. You may want to cuddle after. Vibrators know their place when you shut them down." Mino began walking up the street, leaving him to follow.

Yes, I probably would.

* * * *

Mino yawned and stretched. She'd done more knickknack shopping today than she had in a long time. At least there was chocolate. Swinging her feet out of bed, she padded from the bedroom to the kitchen, where she'd left it on the counter.

Her eyes drifted to Beau's room as she passed it by. It wouldn't take much to go in there and see just how much of what he'd said had been bluster and what was the truth.

"No thank you," she muttered. "That's a bunch of craziness and insanity I don't need to be dipping my toe into."

Not to mention it wouldn't just be her toe — she would jump in willingly, head first. Hell, she had dreamed about him enough that it was hard to turn down the real thing. In the kitchen, she flipped on a light and stared at the array of chocolate.

Reaching for a small box of assorted delights, she turned the light back off, went to the living room and claimed the sofa. She unwrapped the first and popped it into her mouth, then she gasped, a small scream near to flying free.

Beau hopped the back of the couch and landed beside her. "What are you doing up?"

"Eating chocolate and why the fuck are you scaring me like that?"

His fingertips grazed her arm as he searched for the box in the dark. "Who else is in this place with you? No one. Didn't think you would be scared."

If I move the box up, will he brush my breast to find it?

He took one and she gulped when his shoulder pressed tight against her own. Why he had to sit so close, she wasn't sure, but the caramel in her mouth wasn't going to let her ask without sounding like a pig so she kept the question to herself.

"Yuck," he said once she swallowed her piece. "I don't like this one. Here."

Before she could say anything one way or the other, he was pushing the remainder of his bite into her mouth and she opened without a protest. Her lips glanced along his fingers and her belly tightened with need.

While she chewed it, he dug for another one. She didn't see what the issue was with this one. There was a fresh mint crunch in the center. The moment she finished it he had another there and she opened, accepting his offer.

"Why are you biting into them all if you don't like them?" she asked around the nougat center.

"I liked that one. I was sharing with you." His lips were on her cheek, moving with his words, tempting her. Tantalizing her. Torturing her. "Want to give it back?"

The butterflies morphed into a much larger bird, increasing the feeling in her gut. "I've eaten it."

"There are ways to still get the flavor." He moved his face and scraped her skin with the stubble, which only made her want more of that scratchy feel.

"Just eat another."

"If that's what you want."

No, it wasn't, but she refused, *refused,* to be another notch on his bed frame. They settled into finishing up the box, half of each chocolate for each. He fed her and she fed him. It was oddly intimate and had her wishing for so much more. They readjusted on the couch and she had her head on his shoulder while his cheek pressed against her hair.

Never in her wildest dreams had she ever envisioned that she would be curled up on the couch with her dream man, cuddling. He had one arm around her, stroking up and down her exposed skin, making idyllic patterns.

"Did you always want to be a doctor, Mino?"

Sated on the mixture of chocolate and being this close to Beau, she hovered on cloud nine. Sucking the remnants off her fingers, she sighed.

"No. I wanted to be a cop."

"A cop?"

"Yes. I was in love with the shiny badge. Wanted to have one all my own." She closed her eyes and recalled days of running around with a child's badge clipped to her belt, trying so hard to be more impressive than she was at that age.

"So what happened?"

She sobered. "My parents. Told me I didn't have what it took to be one since I cried whenever someone upset me. They told me to try for something else like a stocker in a store so I didn't have to deal much with the public."

"That's bullshit." Anger tinged his voice. "When did you change your mind?"

"I had a childhood friend named Frank. He lived up the street from me. We were both a bit bookish in school and got picked on. I would go to his house after school. His mother had cancer and I began to help her out with some things on her really bad days. I had a knack for it. So I looked up every book I could on medical things and read them." She shifted on the seat. "I read them to her, to Frank, to my stuffed pig, Doris."

His shoulders moved as he chuckled. "Wait. Doris?"

"I couldn't name her Wilbur. She was a girl. Although I really loved *Charlotte's Web*."

"Did she have advice for you?"

"Of course. Go to medical school. Become a doctor and see if you could help people like her. And I wanted to help people like Frank's mom." She pinched the bridge of her nose. "I hid my grades from my parents, not that they were interested. They were shocked I wasn't dropping out."

"So they never came to anything you did in school?"

"Not a one." Funny how it didn't hurt so much anymore to think about their lack of parenting. "Frank's parents did. At least his father when his mom couldn't find the energy to go. They came to everything I did. Hell, they had paid for most of it anyway." The pain of losing the Martins still tore into her, however.

"So they were your parents. Why did you leave medical school the first time?"

Her body was primed to react to that question and did as it always had, tensed. Beau didn't move other than to angle his head to push his lips against her hair.

"Maybe it will lessen if you talk about it."

She doubted it. Tears burned her eyes within seconds. "They were murdered."

"Who was?"

"Frank and his family." Tears leaked from the corners of her eyes and she didn't bother wiping them away.

"What happened?"

"One of their neighbors got drunk and started beating on his wife. Mr. Martin went over to try and help. About ten minutes after he came home, the guy showed up at their door with some of his fucking buddies and shot them all. Even Frank." Her voice shook and he readjusted so his arm settled along her back.

"I'm sorry for your loss. But why didn't you return to school after things were calmed down?"

"By then Masters had found me. In fact, he was the one who was there when I showed up to view the bodies."

"What was he doing there?"

"Never asked him. He just promised he would help me find all the friends of that asshole and bring them to justice."

"And did he?"

"Yes." She burrowed closer to Beau. "I thought it would take away the bitterness and anger I had, but it didn't."

"It made it worse for you."

Beau didn't make it a question.

"How do you know that?" *I wish I could see his face.*

"Because while they were alive you had an outlet for your anger. When that was over and all involved were either dead or arrested, you didn't have anything left to put the rage to. It happens, but you have to let it go, or it will eat you alive."

"I wanted to make them suffer. Is that wrong?"

"No. All that means is you're human like the rest of us."

The topic was getting more serious than she wanted to be with him, so she took the out he dangled and ran with it.

"Are you sure? I thought I was a fairy. Don't make me be human. Or at least a superhero."

His deep laugh set her back at ease, calming the anger that had been churning in her gut once more.

"You're above me, Mino, for damn sure. You soar way above me, but you're still human." He kissed her temple.

She wanted to melt but took it for what it was, a brotherly kiss. Moving the empty box off her lap, she began to rise. He gripped her and pulled her back to him.

"Shh." His hissed order kept the question contained on her lips.

The change in him astounded her. While his body didn't get any harder — not that it needed to — the air around him morphed from something relaxed to dangerous in the time it took him to hush her unasked question.

He chambered a round in his weapon.

Christ, he had that on him this whole time?

"Stay here and stay low," he uttered against her ear seconds before he pushed her down. "Don't move until I come get you."

"Understood," she whispered.

The chill engulfing her the moment he was away from her was from more from just not being next to him. Fear increased it and she lay as still as she could, hoping this would be over soon. Whatever it was.

She considered turning on the light then nixed that. If they were trying to sneak in and search for her, there was no sense in giving them a better look at where she was. Mino thought fast. This was an older couch and she might just be able to slip under it since it was raised off the floor a bit.

I'm down here, but down more should be good. Right? He said stay down. That down is down from this down.

Breathing rapidly, she slithered off the cushions and inched her way underneath the couch as best she could. So long as it remained dark, she should be fine. If the lights had been on, she'd be fucked.

Gunfire rang out and she squeezed her eyes tight. *I don't want to see anything before someone shoots me.*

The heavy thudding of running feet had them flying back open, however. *Is that Beau? Is he shot? Does he need help?*

Fuck. She slithered free from her spot and brought up the layout of this place. She was clear for about ten paces. About to get to her feet, she paused when the floor squeaked behind her.

No way this is Beau. Cautiously, she backed back up under the couch and held her breath. The footfalls were soft, so either the man was light on his feet or it was a woman.

The air thick with tension and she barely breathed as she waited for something to happen. When it did, it was swift.

Three shots and a body thumped to the ground by her. She didn't scream but she did pray that it wasn't someone who was going to turn and shoot her where she was. Lights came on and she blinked in rapid succession, trying to get adjusted.

"Mino?"

The body before her was a younger woman, her face done up with black streaks for added camouflage against her pale skin. The red hair coming from beneath her cap made Mino think about Anabelle Lee.

"Mino?" Beau called for her a second time.

"I'm under here," she called.

The couch was lifted and she scrambled back and got to her feet. With a deep breath, she glanced to the man who'd just moved the object she'd been hiding beneath as if it was made of cotton. He appeared fine.

"We have to move. This was an advance team." He never looked at the dead bodies.

He reached out behind him and she took his hand, allowing him to drag her down the hall to her room. "Get what you need."

"An advance team?" she questioned as she pulled her bag over and shoved her meager items inside it.

"Yes. To make sure we were here. And to try and kill us if possible. They failed. More will come." He appeared in the doorway, a shirt covering his once bare chest and a bag slung over his shoulder with a gun in hand. "Let's move."

She followed him, struggling to keep her questions to herself. He paused at the door to the garage and handed his bag to her. The moment her fingers closed around the straps, he withdrew another weapon. Then he kicked in the door and more shots rang out.

It was official, she much preferred being behind a desk to being in this type of situation. She wanted to lock her knees and not move a muscle.

"Go," he barked.

She did, hauling both bags with her. Tossing them in, she then scrambled in after him.

"Keep your head down and buckle up."

His order was followed by him backing out through the garage door and tearing off down the street as a hail of gunfire followed them.

Yeah, she wasn't cut out for this kind of a life, not at all. Being a cop wouldn't have been her thing, even if her parents had been supportive.

Chapter Seven

Beau sat on the bed while Mino stood between his legs, head bent as she sewed him up from the bullet wound he'd acquired. It stung but he'd had much worse during his time with Theta. Besides, right now he was fine. She was safe and he had her within reach of him. It wouldn't take much for him to pull her close and see where it led.

Her walls had been erected once more. But she worked on his injury with diligence.

"You sure you're okay?" he asked as she tied off the suture.

"Fine."

"Talk to me, Mino."

"Why? Nothing to say about what happened. They wanted to kill us and you didn't let it happen. End of story."

"Bullshit. What's going on?"

"I'm not used to dead bodies like that around me, okay? Allow me some fucking time to process this."

"You work in a hospital, surely you see them there."

"Not freshly shot so they fall directly in my line of sight so it's the first thing I see when the lights come on."

"Sorry about that."

"Whatever."

He hated that tone in her voice but let it go. She stepped back and began gathering up all the bloody gauze and disinfecting pads she'd used on him. He allowed her to move away three steps before he captured her arm in his hand.

"What?"

She wouldn't meet his gaze.

"Look at me."

With a heavy and dramatic sigh, she turned her head in his direction. "Happy now?"

Well no, he wasn't. He released her and stood. She tipped her head back to maintain eye contact.

"Are you sure you're okay?"

Her smile was small and almost nonexistent. "I'm fine. My arm is sore but I'm not the one bleeding. Or wasn't the one bleeding."

"I've been shot before and I'm sure I will be again. Don't worry about me. I'll be fine."

"Of course you will." She tossed the items into the trash and walked back to park herself beside him. "Do you know who they were?"

"No clue. If I had to guess, I would think they were working with Whitney and she may have been following the advance team. Masters sent some people there to find out what they could glean from it."

She trembled next to him and he gathered her close in his arms without a second thought. This wasn't her life and here she'd been shot at more than once within a week. His heart broke when the sob slipped free.

"You're okay, Mino. You've got this."

"How do you get used to it?"

There existed a slight stammer and hesitation in her question he knew she didn't want to have. So he didn't bring attention to it. It was the least he could do.

"I don't know how to answer that. You shouldn't have to. And this is on me for using you as bait."

"It's the way to bring this to an end. I'll deal with it."

He cupped her cheek in one hand and tilted her head to his. Swiping his thumb along her skin, he removed the tears that leaked over. Lost in her gaze, he dipped his head and pressed his lips to hers.

She froze for a second before she melted beneath him, mouth opening to welcome him. He pushed his tongue forward and found hers there, waiting and twining with his. Her moan flowed into him and he brought his other arm around her, mindful of her injury, not giving a damn about his own. With her curves flush to him, his body reacted. Hard. Painfully.

He ran his right hand over her ribs, desperate for skin-to-skin contact. When he reached the hem of her shirt, he inched it up until her warm flesh was beneath his palm. His cock jerked in his pants. Moving up until he cupped a breast, he then flicked his thumb along the taut nipple.

Part of him wanted to take her, rough and fast, just to appease the desperate hunger eating away at him. On the other hand, this was Mino. She deserved so much better than a swift fuck in a rundown motel room.

He nibbled on her lower lip as he ended the kiss, eyes fixed on her face. She slowly opened her eyes when her lip popped from his hold.

"Mino," he began.

"Can you just not talk about this, Beau?"

She moved out of his hold and he let her go. He might be a womanizer and a man-whore according to some, but he wasn't, nor would he ever be, a man who forced himself on a woman.

The more space she put between them killed him a tiny bit more. He wanted her against him, in his arms. Where her heartbeat could be experienced along his body, where her breaths were felt. To have her silken hair brushing his chin and to be surrounded by the scent that was only Mino.

But he didn't move. He allowed her the distance. His cock disagreed with his decision but he ignored it as best he could.

He got to his feet and gestured to the bed. "You should get some sleep. We head out in an hour or so."

She yawned. Fuck, even that was sexy to him.

Mino maneuvered around him and slipped onto the bed before putting her back to him.

At least she trusted him to keep watch. He didn't move until he was confident she'd fallen asleep. It didn't take long. This was wearing her down. Only then did he allow himself to get closer to her once more.

With the memory of the feel of her breast in his hand killing him, what would they be like in his mouth? How about her clit? Would she be a screamer? He would bet so and wanted desperately to find out.

He bent down and covered her with a blanket then retreated to the far corner of the room, with a direct line to the door and a corner of the curtained window to peek out from behind.

Sidearm resting in the open beside him, he pulled out his phone and placed a call.

"Where are you?"

"Hello to you too, Ethan."

"Oh, never mind. I see you."

He could hear his cousin typing away.

"How's Grams?"

Ethan cleared his throat. "Upset but safe. I didn't give her a choice this time. She's staying here with Rally and me. They're out there cooking something together right now."

"Tell her I'm sorry." He rubbed the back of his neck and checked outside again. Still quiet. He also set the alarm on his watch so he would know when to wake her.

"How's Mino?"

"Hanging in there."

Ethan was silent. It wasn't like he talked a lot but this was a pregnant pause. "What did you do to her?"

Tongue down her throat and hand on her breast. "Nothing. Why do you think I would do something to her?"

"Beau, you're my cousin and I love you dearly but this woman is your weakness. Always has been. We have all been waiting for you to see it. And accept it."

He moved his gaze back to the woman sleeping on the bed. *My weakness?*

"Nothing to say about that?"

"No," Beau replied. "You're wrong. She's not my weakness." *Why am I arguing this with him? I've admitted to myself she is. He's my cousin and he knows me almost as well as I know myself.*

"Right, which explains perfectly why you went apeshit the moment you found out she'd quit. And why you refused to go visit her, yet checked up on her all the time, to the extent of knowing her address and how the fuck to get in her place. Why, when this happened, you refused to let Masters send anyone else to keep her safe."

"I was closest."

"And we both know you can move faster without her, yet you're sacrificing speed to keep her with you."

"Who would he have sent? Some new agent? Her life is in danger." He fisted a hand and took several deep breaths.

"New agents are capable of averting coups, saving dignitaries and stopping terrorism. Why do you think they are incapable of protecting one woman?"

"Because she's mine," he growled, furious at the prospect of another man who she relied on for safety being near her.

Ethan coughed again. "And there we have it, ladies and gentlemen. The crux of the reason the great and powerful Beauregard Jackson is doing what he's doing."

"Fuck you, Ethan."

His cousin laughed lightly. "Be easy on her, Beau. She's loved you for years. It won't take much for you to break her." He hung up.

Won't. Not wouldn't but won't, as if Ethan already assumed Beau would break her. He stared down at his hands. Large, strong, scarred. Each time she was next to him, he thought of her as delicate. Well, not even only when she was beside him. Compared to him, she was. Ethan was right—he would break her.

He sat there and thought about it until five minutes before his alarm went off. He turned it off and went to the bed.

"Mino. Wake up."

She did after he nudged the mattress with his boot. With a yawn, she got up and padded to the bathroom. Out of the room moments later, she rolled her shoulders and looked at him.

His heart shattered. So this was what it was like to have something he couldn't have before him, tempting him?

"Let's get moving," he said, voice colder than he meant it to be.

Her gaze narrowed slightly before she nodded. "Fine."

She swiped both bags and waited for him to move. Beau stared into her eyes and didn't see anything but guarded trust. He turned on his heels, leading the way back out to their vehicle, eyes open and remaining alert for anything.

Mino sat in the passenger seat and picked at the cotton material of her pants, pulling off the nonexistent pilling. The tension between her and Beau was thick enough she could chew it. She didn't like it, preferring their easygoing banter and teasing that had been there for years.

I want it to go back to the easygoing bit. I have enough fear right now without having to deal with the tension between us.

Something had happened since that kiss. Her gut clenched as she thought about it. The man knew how to kiss, for sure, but his touch on her breast had damn near made her orgasm. Just to have that rough hand on her hypersensitive skin had been enough. Her boobs had always been a highly erogenous zone for her and it had never been so apparent as it was when he'd touched her.

Night was falling and she moved her body, trying to work out some of the kinks in it. She was stiff, and not in a good way. Her lips kicked up in a smile as she thought about what it would be like to be stiff in a good way.

"What are you smiling about over there?"

His slow drawl wound around her and heated her entire body.

"Thinking how nice it would be if I wasn't stiff from a gunshot but something fun." The words slipped free before she could contain them.

"Is that so?"

I've come this far, why stop now? He's the same man. A friend. Someone I supposedly can joke and pick with.

"It is. I mean, think about it." She settled back into the seat a bit more and stretched out her legs, flexing her ankles. "If you had the choice of being stiff from gunshot wounds or because you had just been a willing participant in a marathon round of sex, which would you choose?"

"Do I get to pick who the sex is with?"

She laughed, thrilled as punch that the ice between them had begun to melt.

"Does it matter?"

"Definitely," he drawled. "Baby, there are some people out there who, if it was my choice, I would much rather take a bullet than have them in my bed."

She pursed her lips. "Interesting."

"What is?"

"I never thought you'd turn down sex."

"I turn it down a lot," he said. "I'm not always in someone's bed."

She picked up on the edge to his tone.

"Sorry, it just seemed that way. I mean, you sent out flowers three times a week minimum. I was always setting up dinner dates for you and mailing out jewelry. Figured you were very busy in that arena." For the life of her, she couldn't come up with a single reason she was apologizing to him.

"You paid attention."

"You made it my business when you couldn't keep it all straight on your own and put me in the middle."

He glanced at her. "You were one hell of a secretary, Mino. More than that, you kept us organized and on point."

"Someone had to." She hid her smile at his praise.

"However," he added, his voice going all professor, "I'm not as much of a whore as y'all make me out to be. I love women, love making them smile. Doesn't mean I sleep with everything that walks in front of me."

"You don't have to justify anything to me, Beau. It's your life."

"I want you to know I'm better than that, Mino."

There went more of that stomach-fluttering thing. He cared what she thought? Shoot her now, she was damn near giddy. She took a deep breath to give herself a moment to get composed.

"I'm sure you are. Grams wouldn't have it any other way."

Yep, that sounded calm and collected. And adult friendly like. Not simpering fluttering moron.

"There is that."

"So, if you don't then why did, or do, you make it seem this way?"

"Better than having my cousins constantly trying to set me up with someone's friend of a friend."

"Makes sense. But now I'm curious about something." The devil on her shoulder woke up and began poking her with its pitchfork.

"Ask away."

"Are you a virgin? Were all those women being bribed to talk about how good you were in the sack?" She bit her lip to keep from laughing. "Is that your big secret?"

He decelerated the car and pulled over to the side of the interstate, as if they were taking a country drive and he wanted a moment, then he angled his body to face her. Cars raced by them but Mino gazed at him, eyes wide.

His entire body vibrated with power and sexual prowess. "You let me know when you want to find out the answer to that question. I'm no virgin and I'm *more* than happy to show you if they were saying that because of a bribe or not."

He'd slowed his unhurried speech even more and it rolled down her skin, setting it aflame. She had to fight to stop from squirming on the seat. Could a voice be sex? Obviously it could, because Beau had that working for him in one hell of a way. He opened his mouth and sex came out. It was the only way she could explain it.

But here again, she wasn't about to back down, so she leaned closer, almost touching him but not. Outside the car, vehicles continued to streak by, shaking them with the force of the wind.

Staring deep into those intoxicating green jeweled eyes, she shrugged. "You had your chance earlier and you ran."

He narrowed his eyes and in the following second she felt like prey locked in the sights of a predator.

Beau placed his index finger beneath her chin, tipping her head up slightly. "Trust me, Mino. I didn't run. I opted to stop. Not an easy decision, believe me. But next time, I won't stop. Next time, I'll show you just exactly what I want to do to you. What I want you to do to me."

Was she a puddle of drool yet? She tried to swallow a few times. It wasn't working well. She had no moisture in her mouth.

"Sure thing," she said, trying to keep the desire and lust out of her voice.

He dragged his finger up and placed it over her lips, traced them then tapped her nose. Then he sat back and got them on the road once more.

Fuck.

Silence existed between them until he got off the interstate and pulled up to another small motel. She groaned.

"What?" he asked, allowing the car to idle.

"Why are we staying here? We know they are after us. Can't we stay somewhere nice where I don't have to worry about the bedbugs carrying me off to be their queen somewhere?"

"I thought every girl wanted to be a queen?"

She punched him in the shoulder. "Ouch, are you kidding me? I can't even hit you without injuring myself?"

"After trying it so many times, don't you think you should know your small hands won't hurt me? Besides, we all learned a lesson in school. Say it with me. Hitting isn't nice, we should use our words," he taunted her.

It worked and she punched him again. And it still hurt a second time. Perhaps even more. This time he captured her hand and pressed a kiss to her knuckles.

The pain melted away, bringing up other feelings she didn't need to be focused on right now.

"Better?"

"If I say no?"

"Then I do this." He kissed each one separately and never once took his eyes off her.

God damn it. The words begging him to take her teetered on the tip of her tongue. She couldn't let them slip free.

"Thank you," she managed to force out as she attempted to take back her hand. "All better now."

"Your call." He released her.

"I'm serious about the motel, Beau. Please."

"We're just renting a room here, not staying. We want them to come here. Not many people and hopefully there won't be casualties. At least not innocent ones."

"We're only, like, two hours from the other place."

"I know."

"That's not typical for you. You wouldn't typically stay in the area knowing your cover has been blown."

"True, but I want them to come again. I'm tired of playing defense. I'm switching to offense."

"Okay. Not following, but let's do it."

"Come on then." He killed the engine and they both got out.

Inside, she hid her disgust with the establishment. No, it wasn't filthy, like dirt on the floor, but it could for sure use a good cleaning. A tall, rangy man walked up from the back and slowed as he looked at the two of them.

"Can I help you?" he asked, his tone barely polite.

Beau slid an arm around her waist and yanked her to him. "Need to rent a room for me and my girl here."

Mino almost stared at him. No southern accent, just sharp, clipped words. She hated it.

"The two of you?" the man took another look.

"Kind of hard to get some screwing accomplished if you don't have a partner. I'm not looking to rent a place to jack off. I can do that in my car, but she wants a bed for sex. So here we are." He adjusted his hat and she wanted to smack it off him.

His answer must have worked, because the man asked for money and slid a key over. On the way out, Beau popped her on the ass and laughed out of the door.

"Really? Did you have to make me out to be a hooker?"

He tsked. "Never called you that."

"It was implied." Not that her impression of this establishment would have improved if he'd called her his wife.

"Look at this place, Mino," he said as they got back into the car to head to the room. "Recognize the name?"

She stared at the sign and frowned. "Elmer's Roadside Palace." The name was vaguely familiar and she scrunched her forehead as she thought. "Shit, this was one of Mansfield's places."

Beau smiled at her. "Exactly."

She nodded. "Offense."

"Precisely. He doesn't know we know of his affiliation to it, but you can be damn sure that man will let him know. He has a big problem with us anyway but will want to stay in the good graces of that psychopath."

"What's that man's issue with you? Me, I could see it all over his face."

"Because I was with you and happy about it. Talking about coitus and the like." He drove them around the corner from the front and parked before their room. "You know I'm not to be fornicating with the likes of you."

She rolled her eyes. "If they know where we are staying, where will we be?"

"Next door. Across would be better but he didn't put us there. So we'll take the door next to it."

"It's locked," she blurted then snapped her mouth shut. "Never mind."

Together, they went into the room and her body cried out for a large king-sized bed with big fluffy pillows, not this uncomfortable-looking double. When he went next door and let himself in, she stood outside the door and kept watch. Not that there was anyone here. Man knew what he was doing, for sure — he'd picked a place that had very few civilians.

I'm a fucking civilian and I'm here.

"Lock the door behind you and come on in."

They were seated in the room next door, lights off, while they waited. After a quick peek out of the window, he looked back to her. "What should we do now?"

"Fuck."

The way his eyes widened in the waning light between them, she realized her word had not just been an internal thought.

'Fuck' was right.

Chapter Eight

Did I hear her correctly? Beau replayed this in his head, more than once to be sure he'd not been hearing things. He came up with the same answer each time. He'd asked her what she wanted to do and her reply had been 'fuck'. His body, completely in agreement with the idea, let him know just how on board it was. His cock thrust hard against his jeans and his palms itched with the need to touch her. Everywhere.

He longed to turn the light on and make sure she wasn't lying, stare into her eyes and have her repeat that single word he'd wanted to hear for so long.

"A quickie against the wall?" He did his best to make it a joke but somewhere in the delivery it fell flat.

Her shadow neared. "If that's what it takes." She touched his chest and spread her fingers wide. "For, like, five minutes, can we forget everything else? I don't think they're going to be just yet."

"Mino," the rasped word fell from his lips.

She put her other hand on him. "Who knows what is going to happen tonight, Beau? We could both die."

Hell no, he wouldn't let that happen to her. He peeked once more. The lot lights were on but nothing else moved out here. He released the curtain and captured her wrists.

"Are you sure about this?"

"I'd really prefer not to dig too deep here, Beau. I'm looking for sex, quick and easy, like."

He yanked her to him. "There will be nothing quick and easy about this, Mino. You need to know that."

"I thought we had to plan on them coming?" Her breathy voice brushed over his lips and he wanted to taste her.

"We do. But first, you plan on it." He claimed her mouth.

She sank into him, wrapping her arms around his neck and pushing up on her toes so their bodies fit tighter together. God, he wanted this woman.

He shoved his hands up beneath her shirt, seeking her smooth skin and full breasts. Her groan filled his mouth when he cupped them. Grasping the points, he tugged on them as she whimpered and squirmed beneath his touch. She nipped his lips and cried out, body shaking.

He dropped his head, took one breast in his mouth, through the shirt, and sucked. Her heart pounded and she dug her nails into his shoulders, near his most recent injury, but he didn't give a damn. So long as she didn't stop touching him, he was fine with wherever her hands went.

He switched to her other breast and gave it the same treatment before he pushed her shirt up over them and tugged her bra down, exposing them to his mouth. When he blew across her nipples, she gasped and shuddered when he flicked his tongue over them, alternating back and forth.

She raked her nails down his side and he lifted her, pinning her to the wall, making it so he didn't have to bend to enjoy her breasts. Mino threaded a hand into his hair and held him tight to her. Her moans and mewls added more blood to his cock.

"Please," she whimpered. "I'm about to come."

Music to his ears. He slipped a hand down into her pants, cupped her pussy and pushed away the edge of her panties, idly circling her clit. Her mewls grew to louder whimpers. He pushed inside her with one finger.

"Fuck," he uttered as she sucked him with her wet heat. "So damn tight, Mino."

She splintered around him, pulling on his hair with painful yanks as she came. The internal walls of her pussy rippled, gripping him and making him wish it was his cock buried deep inside her.

"Beau," she begged, her hips bucking against his hand. "Please."

He undid his jeans with one hand and pulled out his cock. "Get out of those fucking pants."

She released his hair and he supported her as she wriggled them over her ass and, with a bit of fancy maneuvering, freed one leg. Then she hooked it back around him, rubbing her wet pussy along his cock.

He took a final peek out of the window and released the curtain with a groan as she curved her fingers around him and stroked. She moved the head up and down her wet slit.

"Waiting for a written invitation?"

"Guide me in," he ordered.

She tapped his cock against herself three times before putting his head at her entrance. He closed his eyes and pushed forward. Her soft gasp had him wishing once more they could have the lights on and he could watch her. Give him the permission to watch those pupils dilate and widen as he slid deep. Allow him to memorize the expression on her face as he held still, letting her to get acclimated to his size.

"Fuck me," she breathed.

Pinching one nipple, he replied, "I plan on it." He pushed forward until he was seated within her. Then he found her mouth and sucked on her tongue. Her pussy clenched around him and she began moving her hips.

Quick. That word he hated batted around in his mind. This couldn't be long and drawn out. He had to make it fast so they were ready when whoever came showed up. It wouldn't do to be cock deep in her pussy during a gun fight.

Placing his thumb on her clit, he moved it as he began to thrust. Swallowing all her cries, he loved the way she dug into him with her nails, raking them down his back, shredding into his shoulders. She held him like she never wanted to release him, and he was fine with that.

Her heat surrounded him as he worked his hips faster and faster, going as deep as he could within her, needing her to know that after this there wasn't another who would be able to do for her what he was. That she wouldn't be happy with another's touch on her body. He was making her his.

Thank God the wall didn't have any leeway, because he needed the purchase to keep her there. She undulated with him, giving as good as she got. Mino reached past his hand and gripped his cock as he drove into her, giving him more sensation when he withdrew.

"Christ, Mino," he growled against her lips as he thrust hard and held still.

She trembled and he could feel them all through her body. The extra vibrations ripped through his cock.

She angled her fingers so when he pulled back, her nails dragged along his shaft.

"God, more," she pleaded.

Once wasn't going to be enough for him with her. Not in this lifetime. Tugging harder on her nipple, he pinched her clit and pistoned into her as if it were the last time he was ever going to have sex.

The room was full of the slapping of skin-against-skin as he took her. His mouth over hers kept her cries contained. She screamed and arched her back, pushing herself deeper onto his length. He didn't slow as she came around him. Only once she'd stopped did he allow himself to let go.

The blue balls he'd had erupted and he shot deep inside her. Seconds after he came, he realized he'd not used a condom, but that thought vanished in a heartbeat when she shuddered around him once more.

Sweaty and panting, they stayed against the wall for a moment. His kiss became gentle and when he ended it, he didn't move back, but remained close. With their foreheads touching, he smoothed his hands up her sides.

"I bet you look sexy as fuck," he whispered. "One pant leg off, panties wrenched to the side, shirt shoved up under your chin and your bra yanked down, exposing your breasts. I wish I had light to see your kiss-swollen lips and hazy eyes."

"Is 'thank you' an inappropriate comment to make right about now?"

He smiled and kissed her again. "Probably for most people, but I'm me."

"In that case, thank you for that. Experience."

He lifted her away from the wall and carried her in the dark through to the bathroom, where he shut the door and turned on the light. Sure enough, those eyes were still a bit hazy and out of it. Her lips were parted and swollen from his kisses.

"You're fucking gorgeous," he said.

"Not too bad yourself. Why are we in here?"

"Cleaning up a bit. I know we can't shower since this room is supposed to be empty but we can do a bit." He pulled out of her and paused when she reached for him.

"Damn," she said stroking him. "Did it hurt?"

He didn't have to look down to know what she meant but there wasn't any way he was going to miss the erotic image of her hand on his cock. So he did and saw her index finger tracing along the black flame tribal tattoo he had inked on his dick.

"Wasn't the most pleasant thing I've had done." Beneath her touch, he grew hard again. Her slight gasp almost had him taking her once more. "Get cleaned up, Mino. Later we can do this. Right now, I have to get out to the window."

"Right," she said without looking away from his dick. "Clean up."

Before he could say anything else, she sank to her knees and took him in her mouth. He dropped his head back.

Holy fuck.

* * * *

Mino waited as he fought those who'd come to the hotel room. They hadn't taken any chances and had sprayed the room from outside with bullets. She sat cowering—yes, she could admit it—in the far corner of the room while Beau prepared to do what he was so good at and waited for them to stop.

Then he left her there and went next door. A few more shots and some crashing around but she didn't move, nor did she open her eyes. She occupied herself by replaying the sexy time she'd shared with Beau.

He was better than I could have ever imagined. Long and thick. Fuck, even thinking about it had her pussy craving more.

She scrunched smaller and buried her hands in her hair, praying he was safe and she wasn't about to lose him again.

"Mino." He said her name about two seconds before the light flicked on.

Blinking rapidly, she took in the man at the door. Beau seemed fine and he had another man with him who looked as if he'd gone about eight rounds in a boxing ring. Blood ran down his lips and nose. There wasn't any doubt he was going to have one hell of a shiner, either.

She pushed to her feet and ignored the sneer on the other man's face. "Who is this fuck?"

"Not sure, but I thought we could find out. Get that black bag from my pack." Beau kicked the door shut behind him and shoved the man forward. "Sit." He thrust him into the chair and kept his weapon trained on him.

Mino retrieved the bag and handed it to him. "Open it," he said without taking his eyes off the prisoner.

She did and gulped. A group of shiny silver instruments. She wasn't a fool and knew what they were for. Extracting information. The thought of Beau torturing someone sat ill with her. She understood he did it but it wasn't anything she had to like.

"What are you going to do?" She gave him the open pouch.

Beau handed her the gun before he pulled out some zip strips from the bag. Within moments, the man was secured at his wrists and ankles, unable to move.

"Get the truth out of him."

"I'm not going to talk, you fuck," the man sneered.

Beau didn't respond, just rocked the chair back and forward, putting a towel beneath him. "Not as good as plastic but this will work in a pinch." He crouched in front of the man. "Now, we both know how this is going to go. I ask questions, you give me answers and if not, we get to see how long you can hold out."

Mino watched the trussed-up man. From his ill expression, she guessed he'd been waiting for Beau to get snarky back. Anything to take more time. But Beau had not risen to his challenge and set out to do what he believed necessary.

I can't sit here and watch this. I'm a doctor. Or will be. I'm not made to sit here and watch another person get tortured, even if he is here to kill me. Bile rose within her and she did her best to swallow it down. It wasn't easy.

"Get me my phone," he told her and Mino listened, handing it over to him. Beau looked at her with those green eyes. "It's going to be quick. We don't have tons of time. I'm sure the man at the front is waiting for an 'all clear' before he comes back here. But he won't take long. He didn't strike me as a patient man."

She stepped away while Beau placed a call to Masters. She recognized the tone he used with the man. Some days it reminded her of a wild animal that was just about to decide you were better eaten. She didn't know why, but that was what it was like for her.

Masters would have been stupid to believe he had this man under control. And Masters wasn't that by any means. He was cagy as fuck, though. She saw how he manipulated all the Jacksons and the others who worked for him.

Worrying her lower lip, she retreated out of the way and leaned against the wall, arms wrapped around her midsection. Beau snapped his head around and pinned his gaze on her, before moving closer. He offered her the phone once more and when she took it, he cupped her chin.

"You okay?"

"No," she admitted. "This is wrong."

"What they're doing is wrong."

"You can't justify this because he shot at you."

Beau blinked a few times then shook his head. "I'm not. I'm doing so because the fucker shot at *you*." He turned back around.

Mino sank to the floor and put her arms around her ears to block out as much of the sound as she could. When Beau touched her arm later, she refused to look at what he'd done to the man, knowing if she saw it, it would change everything. Forever.

He led her outside and put her up in a big truck. *Belonged to one of those who died, I would guess.* Again, not exactly what she wished to be doing.

All the way around, she was nauseated and wanted off this damn ride. Fast.

He drove them to the main entrance. "Wait here."

She didn't reply, nor did she watch him go inside. She kept her eyes down and played music in her mind. Anything to distract her.

Beau returned in moments. "Masters will have a team here in no time."

Mino exhaled sharply and looked at him. He was still so handsome it hurt, but right now, all she could see was him torturing some man because he'd been following orders from some psycho fucker.

"When will they arrive?"

He shifted into first and turned his head to her. "Within the hour."

"Tell Masters I'll be here and to put me somewhere that I don't have to run or do this."

Beau stiffened. "You want me to call Masters for you?"

She gulped. "Yes. You still have more things to do and I, well, I'll just be in the way and I'm not good at watching this kind of thing."

"I'll keep you safe, Mino."

"That's not the issue, Beau. I know you would. But this isn't my... I just can't... Please, call Masters."

A wall closed down around him as he nodded. "Very well." He withdrew his phone and pressed a button. "She wants you to pick her up. So the men coming to clean need to take her with. I'll stay with her until they arrive."

She focused on her hands laced in her lap, unable to face him.

"Done. They will be expecting you." He drove a bit away, turned them around and parked by the front. "Come on."

This she'd not expected but she still climbed down and trailed him inside. He gestured to a seat behind the counter and she took it while he got back there as well.

She longed to ask where the man was who'd been here previously, but somehow kept that to herself. Each time she looked in Beau's direction he was watching the door, yet she swore his eyes were on her.

No one arrived to check in to the motel before her ride out of there. When they came in — a group of six, four men and two women — she got to her feet. Beau did as well and went to speak to one of the men in hushed tones. She wrung her fingers while she waited.

He turned and pointed to her, raked her with his gaze, then walked out of the door and disappeared into the darkness. Moments later, a vehicle headed out.

Really? That was it? No goodbye? No 'thanks for the fuck'?

Betrayal ripped through her but she reminded herself she was the one who'd asked not to be with him. She rubbed her eyes and walked up to the same man he'd been speaking to.

"Miss Mino, we'll have you out of here in no time. If I can have you go with Daniel over there, he'll get you out and settled in a hotel away from here."

Fingers wringing the color from the strap, she hefted her bag and slung it over her shoulder. "Thank you."

She was introduced to Daniel and followed him out to a black SUV. He held the door for her and she slid into the back. He didn't speak as he got them on the road. All Mino could do was think of Beau. She alternated between self-pity and anger toward him. It wasn't fair — she had the right not to want to be in the middle of all that shit. He didn't have to be mad at her about it.

They pulled into an airport and she climbed out before trekking directly to the waiting plane. She knew the drill, had done it many times traveling with Masters. She was the only passenger other than the two men with guns and the pilot on board when the doors shut and they taxied down the runway.

It struck her, Masters had to have ordered this for her.

The men never spoke to her and the pilot was busy flying, so she got a blanket and wrapped herself up in it. Her body was shutting down, her arm continued to throb and she wanted Beau beside her to cuddle up against.

Waking when the plane touched down, she recognized the airport. The private one Theta Corps used. And waiting outside next to the dark SUV stood none other than her old boss, Masters. Tears welled up in her eyes as a long-legged redhead stepped around from the back of the vehicle. Anabelle Lee.

She dashed the tears away and waited for them to stop. Making her way down the steps to the tarmac, she met their gazes and tried for a smile. Anabelle Lee approached her and gave her a hug.

"Are you okay?"

She nodded. "I will be."

"Is my cousin okay?"

"You know Beau, nothing bothers him."

Intelligent blue eyes met hers and Anabelle Lee cocked an eyebrow. "Right."

"Mino."

She gazed up to Masters. He seemed happier now that he was with Anabelle Lee but she wouldn't ever call the man jovial.

"Thank you for allowing me to use the jet."

He had his strong arms crossed over his chest and dropped them to his sides. "You think that's going to do it?" He grabbed her and pulled her in close, hugging her. "You scared the fuck out of me. Are you sure you're okay?"

Confused by the hug, she drew back and nodded once more. "What's going on? You don't hug? At least not me."

Anabelle Lee kissed her husband on the cheek and smiled. "You're family. Come on, let's get you situated at the safe house. Grams is there so you'll at least have company."

She loved Grams, honestly she did, but staying with the woman whose grandson she'd just fucked wasn't high on her list of things to do.

Masters watched her as if he had something else to say, but didn't add anything more. He got behind the wheel and Anabelle Lee claimed the passenger seat. In the back alone, Mino thought about her time with Beau and how much she missed him already.

It wasn't fair. The sex thing was just supposed to be that one quick fuck to get her mind off the most recent events. But no, every time she closed her eyes, she relived his touch, his scent, the immense pleasure she got from being in his embrace. It wasn't going to be as easy as she'd wished for her to get over that man.

Hopefully he would catch Whitney soon and she could go back to her life.

A life without Beauregard Jackson in it.

Chapter Nine

Beau swore at the radiating pain shooting up from his hand. He shook it while staring at the large hole in the wall he'd just created. The others in the room looked at him in shock and disbelief.

He got it. He wasn't one to show emotion. His way was to carry out his job with cool, calm efficiency. He had a reputation and it wasn't for putting his fist through the wall.

Glaring at them, he stalked over to the table where the layout of the compound had been set at. "Are we ready yet?"

A blonde pushed into his line of vision. He recognized her—Paula. They'd used her a few times and he was glad to see her. He'd not laid eyes on her since she'd had a temporary assignment with Masters.

"Paula," he said with a nod.

"Beau." She gestured off to the side.

"What can I do for you?" he asked when they were out of earshot of the others.

"Is everything okay?"

"My personal life isn't yours or anyone else's business. But yes, everything is fine."

She didn't back down. In fact, she narrowed her gaze. "It is when you're acting out of your normal."

"How do you know what my norm is?"

"Because while we may not all have had the pleasure of working with the almighty Beauregard, we all know your reputation. And this, whatever this is, isn't it. Get your head screwed on straight."

He bit back his retort. She was correct. He couldn't be upset and whining about what Mino did or didn't do right before they stormed this compound in Montana. He had to be on his game. Especially since he didn't have either Anabelle Lee or Ethan with him.

The door opened and in walked Ethan. Beau grinned. Okay, so he didn't have Anabelle Lee. He patted Paula on the shoulder.

"Thanks." He headed over to meet Ethan.

"Good to see you, cuz." Ethan hugged him.

"Likewise. What are you doing here? I thought you were home with the missus."

"And miss this opportunity? The fuck I would do that."

"What about Anabelle Lee? She let you leave without her?"

Ethan smiled. "She's pregnant. Masters absolutely refused to let her go anywhere near something which may give her a hangnail. She's not going anywhere for a while."

"Well, fuck me sideways and give me a beer. That's great for her. I'm going to be an uncle."

Ethan grinned. "Technically, *I'll* be the uncle. You'll be cousins."

"They will love me more." He was happy for his cousin but, even so, he couldn't help but wonder about Mino. How she would look carrying his child, watching her belly swell and round as she housed the baby within her.

"Oh fuck, what are you thinking?"

Beau blinked. "Nothing. Let's get this over with. Time for this group to die."

Ethan held his gaze for a bit and Beau would have sworn he could read the message bubble over his head, informing him exactly what he'd been thinking about. Mino pregnant with his child.

Two hours later, Beau crouched by a wall as smoke billowed overhead. Machine gun fire ripped apart the pre-dawn morning, grenades boomed and people screamed and yelled.

He waited for the tap on his shoulder and when it came, he moved forward, Ethan on his six. Sweeping as they moved, they headed for the elevator in the back. There were short bursts of gunfire while the battle died down.

They opened the elevator and stepped in. Ethan hooked up a device to the keypad while Beau stood guard. Moments later, the doors slid shut and they were dropping.

"You know it's likely they already know what's going on up here and are going to unload a shit ton of lead into here when the doors open."

Beau glanced at his cousin then pointed up. Ethan didn't say a word, just got onto the makeshift step Beau made. Soon enough, they had gone through the panel on the top—it was a bit of a tight squeeze for his shoulders, but he made it.

As they continued down, Ethan looked at him while he checked his magazine and put it back in the M-5.

"Something on your mind?" he asked. *Not that I really want to get into a philosophical discussion with you right now.*

"Just wondering when we're going to talk about what happened with you and Mino."

"Never," he replied, staring through the small grate holes to see the interior of the elevator. He peered up and swore. *This is one hell of a long drop. How did no one know of this?*

"So, beers after then," Ethan said unperturbed.

He didn't have to say anything because they coasted to a stop. Sure enough, the moment the doors started to open, more shots rang out, drilling into the wall they would have been in front of.

Beau met Ethan's gaze and after years of working together, they didn't have to speak, so each took their side and waited for the shooters to step into the elevator. He spied muzzles first and neither of them moved. Not until they could see bodies.

Then they fired and Ethan moved the panel. The second Ethan was back on his trigger, Beau jumped down, ready to fire beyond where they could see. Seconds later, Ethan followed and tapped his shoulder.

He went right while Ethan moved left. Except they couldn't go in those directions. Straight was the only option. So they progressed together, steps in sync with one another as they neared their destination.

One man sat behind the desk at the end of the long room. He wore all white and didn't look at all put out by the fact that two armed men were in front of him.

"The Jackson men."

Weapon raised, Beau sighted on him, just waiting. "You so much as twitch and I'll blow a hole in your head."

"So impetuous. How are we supposed to have a discussion if I can't move?" he wriggled his fingers.

Beau put a bullet into the arm of the chair right in front of those digits. The man jumped, eyes wide. "No moving. I suggest you talk calmly. Which brother are you?"

"Not the one you're looking for, that's for sure." A wicked grin. "But how can you know for sure? You can't because I don't exist in this world. I did for a time. People called me Rolf."

Ethan swore beside him but shook his head and stepped back. Beau knew how hard it was for him to be face to face with the man who had tortured him for all that time.

Beau held his gaze. "Then no one will miss you when you're gone."

"That's not very friendly." There was a calm acceptance in his gaze. That of one who knew he was going to die.

Ethan checked the room for electronics and when he found the computer, he went to it and got to work on pulling all the files he could. Beau cleared his throat when the man shifted in the chair and he froze again.

"Where is he?" Beau asked.

"Where's who?"

"Long day. Irritable. Don't push me." He stalked to where the man sat and jerked him up from the chair.

The beeping was the only warning he had. *The fuck?* His twin had him sitting on a bomb. One that was going to go off in less than ten seconds.

"Move!" he yelled to Ethan.

His cousin didn't wait, grabbed computer and all, and the two of them ran for the elevator. The doors had just closed when the explosion rocked them.

They shared a glance before he hooked his fingers to give Ethan a boost. Jumping up after his cousin, he pulled through and stared up at the cables. Ethan still had the fucking computer open and finally he yanked the drive from it and dropped the laptop back into the elevator.

Debris fell from above and he had no doubt more would be coming. This climb was going to blow.

They shouldered their weapons and each grabbed a cable and began to ascend. Below them, the doors rattled beneath the force of whatever happened behind them. A chain of explosions happened and he worked faster, knowing this wasn't going to end well.

"Here," Ethan barked.

He hopped to the ledge and pried open the door. More smoke billowed in as a large chunk of something ripped past Beau, slicing into his shoulder. Gritting his teeth against the pain, he jumped first to Ethan's cable then to the platform, almost losing his balance when the ground rolled beneath their feet.

Ethan yanked him forward so he didn't career back down into the mess below. They went for their guns the second they regained their footing. Squinting against the dust and smoke flying around, they moved.

When they finally made it outside, they looked around as they slipped into the tree line.

"What the fuck?" Beau gasped. "I know the man was insane but strapping his own twin to a bomb? That's just an entirely new level."

As they watched, the entire place went up. Beau stumbled to the radio.

"Sit rep," he said into the device.

As responses came in, he noticed one person who'd not checked in.

"Paula? What's your status?"

Nothing.

He and Ethan started back down. "What's your status? Respond, Paula."

He broke into a run and they got to the spot they'd entered, where a lot of their people had gathered.

"Anyone lay eyes on Paula?"

All he received was negative on that front. Staring at his cousin, he pointed to the men there. "See to the evac, get those injured looked at. And get on that drive, maybe we can find Whitney and Trevor or whoever it was that got out."

"Be safe."

Beau gave a sharp nod, before he delved back into the chaos. He wasn't about to leave anyone behind.

* * * *

Mino smiled at Grams, who was quilting in a living room chair. "I'm getting some tea. May I bring you any?"

"That would be lovely," she said with a smile.

Mino trotted off to fix their drinks. As she waited for the water to heat, she grabbed the mugs and tea bags. Earl Grey for herself and peppermint for Grams.

Staring out of the window, she thought about Beau. No word from him. Nothing about him either. And it bugged her.

"He's fine."

Mino turned. "Excuse me?"

"My grandson. You're concerned about him. He's fine."

"Um, okay."

Grams gave her a small smile. "You think I don't know what's going on between you two?"

"I don't think I know what's going on between us so not sure how you can know."

She gave her a look that had to be patented by every parent. "Because I'm much wiser than either of you." Grams got two spoons from the drawer. "I've quilted for each of my grandchildren. The designs reflect who they are and who they will be. Ethan's fit him and Rally perfectly. So did Anabelle Lee's. These things talk to me, they tell me what to put on them. Quilts are magic."

Mino cocked an eyebrow. *Magic? Really?*

"Beau's is a perfect blend of the two of you."

"I'm not the one for him," she said with a small shake of her head. *I'd love to see what this quilt looks like, though.*

"Because he was a whore for so long?"

Thank God she'd not had any tea in her mouth or it would have been all over the woman. As it was, Mino choked a bit and had to blink away the tears. "I'm sorry, did you just call your grandson a whore?"

"He was one. With a different woman all the time, never settling down. Of course that's because none of them were right for him." She took a deep breath. "But you are."

Mino pushed a hand through her hair. "Are you sure we should be discussing this? I mean, this really isn't any of my business."

"Please," she said dismissively. "This is more about you than you're ready to accept."

The kettle whistled.

"I'm not the woman for him."

She took the water from the stove and poured it into the cups. "Why do you say that?"

"Because it's not our relationship, nothing about us says anything long term. And honestly, I don't believe he's ready to settle down. He's enjoying his life as it's going right now."

"And what about you?"

Mino accepted the cup slid to her. "What about me?"

"Are you okay with him not being in your life?"

"He's not in my life, ma'am. He's not a person I have the choice to make with."

Grams sighed and rolled her eyes. "You young people don't know what you have even when it's right in front of you. Do you think for a second I wouldn't take more time with my James if I had the chance?"

"With all due respect, ma'am, this isn't a wonderful marriage that we want to continue. Beau and I were colleagues and barely that. I was someone he got to try and order around."

The woman stared at her with vivid blue eyes, sharp and brimming with intelligence. "Is that what you truly think? About Beau?"

It doesn't matter, it's how I was made to feel with your grandson. Except for that mind-blowing sex we just shared. During that moment, I felt important to him, but the fact it was so easy for him to let me go after just once again reminded me where I stand in his mind. "Just giving you the facts."

"Facts? Let's talk about that. One, since you arrived at his job, he cut down on the women he was out with. Sure, he still talked a big game, but he didn't go out with half of them. He always had nothing but good things to say about you to me. And that's the most telling of all—he mentioned you to me when we were alone."

She drank her tea and put down the mug. "No offense, ma'am, but he brought Whitney to see you. So maybe it doesn't mean as much as you want it to mean. Excuse me." Mino turned and left before she got snippy with a woman who didn't deserve it.

She was sitting in her room, staring out at the Georgia landscape, when a knock came to her door.

"It's open." She glanced at her watch, noting that two hours had gone by since she'd talked to Grams.

Masters stood in the door and hesitated before he entered the rest of the way.

She waited for him to sit before she asked, "Well? What's going on?"

"Whitney wasn't there. They got one of the twins but the other wasn't there either. He was injured but he's fine. We lost Paula."

She leaned forward, mouth open. "Paula? Damn it. What happened?" He gave her a look and she swore. "Fine. Don't tell me. What happened to Beau? And I don't want to hear any shit about me not being in TC anymore so I can't know."

"I can't share particulars with you, Mino. You know this. He is okay, trust me."

She wanted to scream at the man in front of her, but it was her fault. She was the one who'd left Theta Corps, not the other way around.

"Can I go home now?"

"No."

She accepted that for half a second.

"No? What do you mean no?"

"Whitney is still out there."

She threw her hands up then flopped back.

"Oh, for fuck's sake. I'm tired of waiting for her to come out. She wants me to get to Beau. Fine, use me. Put me out there. Give me the phone I used when she found me the first time." Masters shook his head. "No arguments. I'm tired of putting my life on hold. We nearly had her in Montana but she got away. Let's do it again. Or give me her number because I know you're tracking her cell for when it comes on."

Masters handed over his phone and she did what she'd done in the past, let herself into the information provided by Theta Corps as she was the top man's secretary. Memorizing the number, she pulled out a burner then punched it in.

"This is a bad idea," Masters stated.

"Hush. It's ringing."

"Like my ears'll be when Beau boxes them."

She ignored him. No answer so she left a message. "Whitney. This is Mino, the one you tried to kill in Albuquerque. I'm tired of hiding. Call me so we can set up a time to meet. Just you and me in a public place so you don't blow my head off before we talk." She hung up. "There. I'll let you know when she makes contact."

Mino packed her bag, shaking her head — she still had shit for personal items with her. "Keep Grams safe." She held out her hand and Masters stood.

"I'll drive you."

They walked out in silence. She didn't even say farewell to Grams. Rude? Perhaps but she wasn't looking forward to more scrutiny by that woman who saw far too much.

They left the driveway and he headed down the road. "You know he's going to lose his shit, right?"

She didn't even pretend not to know who it was he was speaking about. "Why are so many people concerned about how Beau and I are getting along? So what if we fucked, he's not going to care any more than he gives a fuck about the others he sleeps with."

She slapped her hand over her mouth and closed her eyes. With a deep breath, she peeked over to Masters. His expression could have been carved out of stone for all the emotion she saw there.

He looked at her and lifted one dark eyebrow. "Feel better?"

"No, not really. I want my damn life back."

"He's not going to be happy, Mino. Regardless of the stuff I'm going to pretend I didn't hear, he isn't going to like you putting yourself back in danger, especially without him there to protect you."

"You said he was hurt."

"That man would be there short of death and I'm not even sure that would keep him from being there."

"Then call him in when I get the location and time."

"You know we handle these things."

She nodded. "I know. And I'm grateful you're going against the norm to let me do this. I just can't keep this up. I swear, I don't know how those people you help handle it."

"They don't have a choice," he reprimanded.

"Look, I was dragged into this because she has a beef with Beau."

"Beef? Isn't she an ex? There's more than that."

"Whatever. Point is, I need my life to be mine again. I don't want to miss school. I need to be able to check on Todd's mother and make sure she doesn't need anything."

Masters took her hand. His dwarfed hers, he was such a large man. However, his touch was gentle and when he squeezed she smiled back at him.

"You are family, Mino. That's the only reason we're going along with this fucking scheme. I want to do like Beau does and lock you away. We love you and want you around."

"I think that's the nicest thing you've ever said to me."

He shrugged. "I'm an asshole. Annie tells me that all the time. It's the truth. But I hate you left thinking I hated you and didn't need you. I did and I do but I understand this is not your calling to be my secretary, or administrative assistant, however you want to call it."

She tightened her grip on him for a brief moment. "You've changed, Masters. I like it. She's good for you."

He parked them at a dealership. "She is. Like he's good for you. Come on." He was out of the car before she could comment.

Within thirty minutes she had a new car, well, a new used car at her disposal. Masters walked her to the door and held it for her.

"We cloned your cell so we'll mobilize when she calls. Keep her in this state so we can make sure we get there in plenty of time."

As if on cue, her phone rang.

"Hello?"

"This evening at four. Food court at Lenox Square. Don't fuck with me on this or there will be hell to pay."

The call ended and she looked up to Masters, who was on his phone. "Go. We'll be there. You won't see us, but we'll be there."

Nerves a wreck, she climbed behind the wheel of the Hyundai Genesis and started the engine. She would have to make sure she didn't lollygag about to get there in time. Putting it into gear, she then drove away with a wave, her mood a mixture of concern and gratitude that this was about to be over.

Chapter Ten

"When this is over, you and I will be having some words," Beau snapped at Masters.

The man appeared unimpressed and unconcerned with the threat just leveled in his direction. He crossed his arms and leaned back in his chair. "My decision. You don't like it, sit it out. Good thing about being in charge is I get to do what I want."

God, he wanted to punch his brother-in-law in the face, more so than usual, but he didn't. Aware of Anabelle Lee's pregnancy, he had no wish to make anything more stressful for her and having—as she considered them—her guys argue was always a sure-fire way to upset her.

"I'm not sitting this out. I'm not staying in this fucking donut truck. I want inside." Where he at least had a chance to get to Mino if she needed him. Not out here across the motherfucking parking lot where she'd be dead fifty times over before he could even get to the door.

"Whitney knows what you look like, she can't be made aware."

"Not my first rodeo, Masters," he growled.

"Then act like it." There wasn't any give or sympathy in the man's voice.

"I'll go where you put me, just have me in there."

"Fine, you go to the top and keep an eye out there."

Beau thought about it, where he would be in relation to the food court. He would make sure he had a clear line of sight to the area and have that bitch Whitney in his view. If she made even a hint of a move toward Mino, he'd kill her, without batting an eye.

Without responding, he walked away and went to find his vantage point. This wasn't how he preferred to do his job. He was more down in the trenches and hands on.

He had his glasses on, which acted like binoculars without appearing any more than regular eyewear. Resting his arms along the barrier, he gazed about like so many others there who came to the mall to people-watch.

Dipping his head, he adjusted the zoom by touching the earpiece where it connected to the lens. The people seated around tables, eating, and laughing, were ones he wasn't interested in. But he didn't see the woman he was.

"She's entered the building."

His body tightened.

"Red shirt, blue jeans and boots." Trevor's voice was cool and impersonal. Not at all as if he and Mino were friends.

Beau thought about it. She had a lot of people there at Theta Corps who liked spending time with her and never had a bad word to say about her. Except him. He could say a bad thing about anyone. *Christ, I'm an ass.*

Sure enough, Mino walked into view. She wasn't moving like anyone who was scared or frightened. No, he detected more anger in her steps. She didn't walk that hard.

He shook his head and watched her move along the floor until she found an open small round table. Taking her seat, she gazed about then settled back before getting up once more. Three minutes later she returned, this time with a drink in her hand. She retook her seat and waited.

Mino fidgeted and Beau wanted to tell her to calm down, that she was being watched and protected. He tightened in on her face as he'd moved to where he could see her profile. She had her hair in a French braid, the barest hint of red gloss on her lips, and earrings that dangled and swayed with each movement she made, no matter how subtle it was.

"Target acquired."

He took a deep breath and waited for further information. Like where she was coming from and what she was wearing. As it came to his ear, he scanned about. Anger surged forth when he watched Whitney walk in.

"No way she's that cocky if she's alone. She's got people here as well." Beau ran his gaze over her, picking out two weapons on her body.

Her sweet smile turned his stomach. She reached out and gave Mino a hug that he knew was a cover for checking for wires and weapons. There were none to be found.

He didn't have audio but he could read lips.

"What is it going to take for you to leave me alone?" Mino questioned.

"I want Beau and you seem to be the best way to get to him." No hiding the hate there.

"You overestimate this power you seem to think I have over him. He doesn't give a damn about me, not any more than he does any woman."

Okay, that hurt. Done for the purpose of getting Whitney or not, he hated those words from her lips.

"I think you're wrong."

Mino shrugged. "I don't give a fuck. Look, I just want to get back to school so what can I do?"

She slid a phone across to Mino. "Call him."

Mino pursed her lips and drummed her fingers on the table before Whitney gestured at her once more.

"And say what?" she asked, picking up the phone, spinning it in her fingers.

"That you want to meet him."

She pursed her lips. "When and where?"

Beau didn't wait to hear any more. She wanted him, she would get him. He was sure it was not how she wanted it and not how Masters wanted it, but he didn't care. He moved along with the flow of the crowd, blending in despite his size.

He had found a quiet place when his phone rang. "Hello?"

"Beau?" Mino sounded unsure.

"What can I do for you, Mino?"

"Can we meet?"

"Sure. What do you need?" *That's it, baby, play it cool. You're doing fine.*

"Just want to talk about...about what happened between us."

"Time and place, I'll be there."

"Where are you at?"

"I'm in Atlanta."

"Atlanta? Okay, how about Centennial Park in an hour?"

"I'll be there, Mino. Promise."

He hung up and continued making his way down.

Standing at the edge of the food court, he watched the two women. They stood together and left the area. He neared them.

No way he was letting Mino into her vehicle. Moving swift, head down, he got closer and closer until he could hear them.

"I don't know why you think I have to go. We came to meet. I've done what you asked. Let me go."

"No. He's going to be much more malleable if we have you with us."

"We?" Mino asked, voice going high.

"I don't trust Theta Corps. They're going to set something up, so you're going to be my bargaining chip."

"Then why did you come here alone if you think they will be doing something?"

Good question. He moved between the rows of cars, eyes locked on where he would take Whitney. Behind that large conversion van.

"I'm not alone. I have men inside. They are looking out for your people and I have a mole inside Theta Corps. For being new, she's damn good."

"You put someone in my old position," Mino stated.

"How do you know she's the secretary?"

"Because that's the only new position recently."

"Not true, you have the opening for a field agent. You lost that blonde bitch Paula."

Her gasp informed Beau that while she knew the news, she was acting as if she'd not heard yet. The women moved past the van, Whitney closer to him than Mino. He snagged her, dragging her behind the vehicle and clamping a hand over her mouth to keep her from alerting those with her.

Mino stared at him, eyes wide. He beckoned to her. She stepped closer.

"You're here," Mino said.

"Where else would I be?" He angled his hip in her direction. "Call Masters and give him the update."

"What update?"

"That I have her."

He gritted his teeth as she slipped her hand inside his pocket. God, he wanted her hands on his bare skin. All over. Touching, exploring, caressing.

"You and I are going to have a discussion, Whitney." He cut off her air until she slumped unconscious against him. Scooping her up in his arms, he beckoned to Mino. "Come with me."

She walked and talked near him. Beau put Whitney in the back seat of his vehicle, zip strips on her wrists and ankles. Then he faced the woman beside him.

"You and I are having a chat once I finish with her."

Mino's smile was sardonic. "Sure, always after you deal with another woman. I never come first. No thank you. Goodbye, Beau." Mino pivoted around and strode away.

He took two steps after her and found Masters in front of him.

"I'm pretty sure I gave you specific orders, Beau." He crossed his hands, glancing pointedly between him and the woman in the back seat. "And this wasn't one of them."

"I wasn't letting Mino get into that vehicle. I have a discussion to have with someone. Excuse me."

He peered around Masters but Mino was no longer in view. Behind the wheel, he backed out of his spot and drove away, a specific destination in mind for this particular discussion. When it was cleared up, he would track Mino down once more.

And he had no plans on letting her go this time.

* * * *

Mino pushed up from the ground, allowing her hand to trail over the grave marker one last time before she dusted off her knees. Her bouquet of mixed flowers lay before it, adding new color.

"I miss you, Todd."

She dashed away her tears, turned and froze. Beau stood there, blue jeans, green and gray flannel shirt, ball cap and his cowboy boots. His thumbs were hooked in the belt loops, directing her attention to the bulge in his jeans. Not like she needed help to focus there.

Hunger flowed through her, as if someone had turned on the spigot and let it run free. Grinding her back teeth, she wiped her hands off on her pants before picking up the dead flowers she had come to remove.

"What do you want?"

"We need to talk."

"So you track me down in a cemetery? Wanna have the conversation right here?" Snark and bitchiness leaked from her tone.

I missed him so fucking much. It's not fair.

"I came to pay my respects as well. Despite whatever you may believe, Mino, I had no wish for him to get caught up in this."

"You didn't even know him. He was what you refer to as a non-person. Not someone integral to your operation or to your bedroom. Not that it matters, for that's the issue, isn't it? People around you get hurt whether you mean for them to or not."

"Does it help?" he asked, closing in on her.

"Does what help?"

"Being a bitch."

She tightened her grip on the dead stems and they bent in her hand. "For sure."

"Here or somewhere private, Mino?"

"Right, because this is such a bustling metropolis." She gestured around them.

"You want to have an argument in the middle of a cemetery? I'm fine with it but I was thinking you may want to be out of public eye."

"Here's fine."

She refused to take him back to her place because she knew exactly where they'd end up if she did that. Bed.

Would that be such a bad thing?

Of course not, but she couldn't afford to let her emotions get involved with him again. While she'd enjoy every moment with him in bed, on the couch, wherever they ended up having sex, afterward would be the hate and anger at herself for giving in once more.

She'd already forgotten herself and had unprotected sex with this man. Not something she needed to do again. A baby wasn't at all on her list. At least not now.

"Suit yourself." He stopped when he stood right in front of her. Eyes locked on each other. Not speaking.

"You have something to say?" she quipped.

His stare was unnerving, as if he were peeling back her layers of protection to see her. The real her. The one who longed to jump into his embrace and kiss him. The her who wanted him to kiss her. Lay her back and make love to her. Hell, even thrust her against a nearby tree and fuck her until she couldn't stand or speak. She wanted sore muscles, raw throat, sweaty bodies. Marks from his lips and scruff on her body.

"You make me insane, Mino," he growled at her.

"I hear they have therapy for that. I happen to know for a fact that Theta Corps offers such things. Go there, talk about your deepest darkest fears."

He knocked back his hat, raked his fingers through his long hair, and shoved it back on his head. "You don't have anything to say to me?"

"Nope."

An entire litany of words pushed against her lips, which she kept sealed. She wasn't going to do this. Not right now, right here, and not with a man who had more women trailing after him than she could ever count.

"What we shared," he began.

She shook her head. "Nope, I changed my mind. I'm not doing this at all. Look, we fucked. Leave it at that. You got another notch on your bedpost. Congrats. Leave me alone, Beau. Go to your – "

"Beau! Are you coming?" a woman called out.

Cold settled around her. She tipped her head to the right, to see around those wide shoulders. A trim brunette was hurrying across the maintained ground toward them. Her dress appeared painted on and her heels weren't made to be traipsing around a graveyard.

Not one, but about fifty knives tore into her heart, shredding what was left of it to tiny little pieces. Biting the inside of her cheek, she fought not to scream and rave. It was always one thing to be the person taking the high road and letting someone off the hook. But it was entirely different when smacked in the face with the fact the other person has already moved on, reminding her how little she meant to him in the first place.

Forcing a polite smile on her face, Mino gestured. "To her."

The woman stopped beside them and smiled. "Are you coming? We're going to be late. Or rather I am." She slipped her arm through his.

Mino allowed herself one more perusal of his form, memorizing it. The woman with him was back in the pattern he usually went out with. Rail thin, fake boobs and bleached teeth.

"Thank you for coming to pay your respects," Mino said softly. "Goodbye."

She walked around the couple and headed for her new vehicle. The Hyundai that Masters had bought for her. She liked the car and he'd said she could keep it. So she had It had been sent out to New Mexico for her.

Tears burned her eyes as she drove out of the lot and back to her hotel room. She was here for another night then would be heading home to her place. Correction, her new place. Masters had also insisted she move to a more secure location. While she'd listened, she'd still kept a small space—she didn't want a large place to clean. She didn't have the time. Or the desire.

She took a small meal in her room then tried for a nap. It was late in the afternoon when she woke to a knocking on her door. Yawning and rubbing her eyes, she padded to the door and pulled it open.

Sleep vanished in a puff and she gulped much-needed air. Beau stood there. She didn't move back, keeping her place and appearing as nonchalant as she could.

"What do you want?"

"We need to talk." He frowned. "Are you okay? Were you sleeping?"

"I'm fine and yes I was sleeping. There's nothing for us to talk about, Beau."

He searched her face with his green eyes. Her belly clenched and flipped under his intense scrutiny. When he nodded, she exhaled, trusting she'd gotten her point across.

Her mistake.

The second she relaxed slightly, he moved. This was the Beau people didn't want to meet. The one who lulled them into a false sense of security with his laid-back easygoing manner. Then he struck faster than a snake.

He lifted her in his arms and entered the hotel room, his mouth on hers with a scorching possessiveness she'd not known he had within him. His tongue plundered her mouth without quarter.

There wasn't power within her to resist him, despite the knowledge that she should. What could one last time hurt?

With her mind made up, she wrapped her arms around him tight, kissing him back. Craving more. Needing him against her. The brush of his rough hands skimming her skin. The scratch of his stubble along her inner thighs or neck.

She grabbed at his shirt, yanking up the back, until he got the message and put enough space between them to rip it off, one-handed, in that way guys always made look so hot. Then they were connected again, lips, skin, hands. Souls.

They thumped around the room, moving from wall space to wall space, devouring each other. Her heart pounded and still she wanted more.

Finally, in the bedroom, he dropped her on the mattress and shed the rest of his clothing before she even stopped bouncing. He covered her, pressing her deep into the thick coverlet.

He didn't speak. Not verbally. He said it all and more with his hands, lips, and eyes. Despite the near angry way they were going at it with each other, she felt his emotion. The intense way he watched her, the overwhelming desire she witnessed in his own expression. The raw, painful need he couldn't hide from her.

While she removed her shirt, he divested her of the lounge pants and underwear. She lay naked before him naked. His possessive stare heated her to near boiling. She bit her lower lip as he grabbed his cock and stroked himself, while he maneuvered between her legs.

Mino gasped, arching her back as he slid home with one steady thrust. He captured her hands, laced their fingers and stretched them out over her head. She let him do as he wished.

Back and forth he moved, filling her, withdrawing and doing it all over again. She hooked her legs high around his waist, wanting him as deep as he could be. He held her wrists and moved his other hand down her body, teasing her nipples and massaging her breasts. She squirmed and bit back the begging. Her moans grew with each deep stroke from him.

When he placed the calloused pad of his thumb against her clit, she gasped. He moved it in small circles, heightening her pleasure with each swirl of movement. Her body burned, desperate for release.

Through the entire thing, he watched her, never taking his eyes off her.

She exploded beneath him, coming hard with a cry. He pumped and kept rubbing her clit. Goosebumps popped up as she struggled to find her breath. Beau pulled out and she stared at his cock, covered in her cream. He flipped her over onto her knees. She kept her butt high and moaned when he nipped one globe.

Mino shook her ass and angled her head to see what he was doing. Before she could focus on him he swiped his tongue up her slit.

"Ah fuck," she cried, bucking back into him.

He grabbed her ass and licked her pussy until she came, trembled and could hardly see straight. After her second orgasm, he pushed back inside her. Slowly, inch by inch, until he could go no farther. Then he sat there. Not moving.

Her sensitive nerves were going haywire. Her muscles screamed in pleasure as did every other part of her. He wrapped one arm around her, drawing her against him tighter, hand drifting back down over her clit and teasing the nub.

Everything else faded away. All she knew was his touch. Time and time again, he carried her up to just before the edge, then brought her back. Over and over. Her throat burned it was so raw from her cries and the begging. Her muscles were taut and burned. She didn't care. *More,* her body cried. *More.*

"More," she croaked out.

His response was a brush of lips along her lower back. She tightened her muscles around him and he growled in response. A few more thrusts and, with a loud groan, he spilled his seed into her. His larger body covered her and bore her down into the mattress.

Perfect.

She had nothing left. Grabbing at his hips when he began to move off her, she encouraged him to stay as he was without a sound. Well, mostly how he'd been. He rolled them over on their sides, so his weight was off her. A pity, because she liked that feeling. Regardless, he held her tight. What she wanted. And she drifted off to sleep thinking about what she'd just done.

For a final mistake, it wasn't a bad one. One more time with Beau. I don't see a downside.

Chapter Eleven

"What's the matter?" Ethan asked as they rode along in the Jeep, heading for the airport. Not an official airport but more like a shack along a landing strip.

"What makes you think anything is the matter?"

Beau stole another glance behind him at the man they'd been sent to apprehend. Lamas Stiegler. International gun runner and most recently having been reported as working with Trevor Mansfield. *Can't the bastard ever just die?* Lamas was still unconscious so he glanced back to Ethan.

His cousin had recovered well from his time as a prisoner. He'd regained that weight they'd been concerned he wouldn't get back. And a bit more muscle than previously. Being married to Rally had also helped. That princess loved his cousin with a passion he hadn't thought existed in the world. Now he saw that same amount with Anabelle Lee and Masters.

I feel that for Mino.

"Because, even for you, you've been quiet. Even Valentino noticed."

"I'm fine."

"Bullshit. You're about as fine as that fuck behind us."

His lips twitched and he scratched at the growth on his jaw. "Rally know you're checking out guys now?"

Ethan flipped him off and got them around the corner before he said anything else. "How's Mino?"

Okay, so it may not be kosher to kill his cousin but right then, the idea had so much merit it wasn't funny. Beau struggled to keep his frayed composure, but when Ethan chuckled, that attempt went right out of the fricking window. Or the space where the window would have been, had it been rolled up. He was fine with everything else but the mere mention of Mino put him instantly on edge and combative.

"How would I know?" he asked, working hard to keep his voice toneless.

Ethan glanced at him and Beau gestured back to the road. "Damn it, keep your eyes forward. This isn't I-75."

"Really?" Ethan rolled his eyes before putting them back on the road. "I didn't know that." He made a big production of looking around. "Where the hell are we then? I took a wrong turn."

"Fuck you," he muttered.

They were traveling along the Sichuan-Tibet Highway in China, a road prone to rock slides, avalanches and shitty weather. If they went over, it was a long way down.

"Want to drive, you big baby?"

Beau nodded. "Yes, in fact I would prefer it."

"Tough shit, you pussy. Give up some of your control, Beau. Embrace it. I'm enjoying this road and I'm going to keep driving." Ethan's grin was diabolical.

He looked at the clouds off in the distance. They needed to be off this road by the time the rain arrived. He bit back the need to point that out to his cousin.

"You're a gargantuan pain in my ass."

"Then I've accomplished what I needed to. None of which tells me what the hell is going on with you and Mino."

"When did you go and turn into Dr. Phil?"

They skidded around a corner, the muddy road making it more difficult to keep a smooth drift. "It's my side gig. You know we're always being told to have a hobby. Mine is this, delving into your personal life."

"Nothing is going on between us."

"Really? Is that your final answer?"

Beau clenched his jaw. It would be bad form for him to punch his cousin and toss him from a moving vehicle. *Right?* In this instance yes, as his cousin was driving. "Drop it, Ethan."

"You know, you should be happy it's me instead of the pregnant viper asking you."

He shuddered at the thought of being caught in a confined space with a pregnant Anabelle Lee. "True."

Viper was putting it mildly — Anabelle Lee had taken to coming unhinged in the space of a second, going from happy to crying uncontrollably to wanting to kill. And that wasn't an idle threat coming from that woman.

"I'm serious, man. I know we don't do the feelings thing and that's fine but I am worried about you. You're not yourself."

"She wants nothing to do with me."

"Give her time. Right now, you're what she associates losing her friend with."

Another check on their prisoner. "No, that's not it. I fucked her."

Beau tightened his hold on the door, biting off a litany of curses when the Jeep slipped and flirted with danger as it almost went off the road. Eyes wide, he glared at his cousin, who righted them and took them to safety around the next corner.

"I'm sorry, you what?"

He cracked his neck. "You heard me just fine." He pinched the bridge of his nose and sighed. "She's not like everyone else. I can't just push her out of my mind. I'd been delusional to think I could in the past. But the second I touched her, that first time I kissed her, everything in my world changed when it came to her. I'm possessive, I want her with me and I'm not even close to being ready to let her go."

Ethan didn't speak for a bit and Beau looked over at him.

"What? Nothing to say now?"

"I'm still wrapping my head around the fact you slept with her. Or trying to." He whistled. "I mean, there were sparks there between the two of you but I thought they were on her end. You never treated her any different than you did someone you viewed as a sister."

"Trust me, there is nothing sisterly about how I feel for her."

"Does Anabelle Lee know?"

"Hell no. I'm not telling her either. Neither are you." Ethan's grin turned wicked and Beau flinched when a shaft of fear hit him. "I mean it, Ethan. If you don't want me to make Rally a widow, you'll keep your mouth shut on this."

His cousin wasn't the least bit threatened. "You better tell her before Mino does." Ethan downshifted and took another corner, the ass of the vehicle fishtailing in the sliding mud. "She finds out after the fact and you'll have to go into protective custody. Hell, that was before she got herself knocked up. She's even more volatile now."

Truth.

"What's the problem then, cuz? So you like her. I don't see the issue?"

"The part where she wants nothing to do with me."

Ethan began laughing. "I know this is difficult for you to think about since you're so used to women falling over themselves to get stuck by your supposedly magical dick, but you may have to try a bit of romance with her."

"She says she doesn't want to be another notch on my bedpost. And it is magical, that's not rumor."

Ethan chortled. "Your bedposts are all cut up, there's not anything left of them to put notches on. But, that being said, I get where she's coming from. You have a reputation. One you made for yourself and one I'm sure you're proud of. But she isn't like everyone else."

"Ain't that the truth."

Ethan cleared his throat and slowed to take a particularly sharp corner. "Point being, you have to show her you're not looking for the next easy pussy to come around. You want her and no one else."

"She should know that." He crossed his arms.

"Don't be a fuck," Ethan bit off. "You have barely been seen with the same woman more than once. Rare occasions, you'll pull out a good fuck buddy to go see but normally you're working your way through this black book of pussy you have somewhere."

"Women like me."

"Nothing wrong with that, but Mino's not going to be one of them. She wants a man who will be true to her. You know she has low self-esteem issues."

"I don't see it. She shouldn't have them."

"Be that as it may, she does. So she's not going to be in something where she's going to be hurt in the end, Beau. She cares for you, that's obvious, but she's protecting her heart."

"What the hell, did you start reading Cosmo in between missions?"

"I've always been more in tune with the women than you. You use them and leave them. I talk to them."

"Fine. Can we please talk about something else? Football? Hockey?"

"All part of your problem, scared to talk about your feelings."

Beau glared at his cousin. Ethan just laughed and asked the Jeep for a bit more speed as the first raindrops fell. Beau didn't respond, wanting Ethan to do what he had to in order to keep them on this damn road.

As they continued down, all he could think about was Mino and their last liaison. No protection. No loving words. Just fucking and he had been gone. Or, rather, she'd been, for she'd snuck out before he got up and never returned to her hotel room.

He and Whitney had had a one-on-one due when he got back but after that, he was putting in for some time off and heading out to New Mexico. Time to make his intentions clear to one stubborn woman.

* * * *

"You have a visitor, Mino, at the front desk." Charlie passed along the information as he walked out of the changing room.

She rubbed the back of her neck. She wasn't in the mood. "Who the fuck comes to a hospital to visit? Thanks, Charlie."

His wave was the only response and she sat on the nearest bench with a groan. Nearing the end of her rotation, she'd been up for well over twenty-four hours. The door swung open, allowing another colleague entrance. This was Manuel. Tall, handsome and damn good at his job. Problem was, he knew it.

"Thought I might find you in here," he said, his patented grin in place.

"Bad form for me to change out in the waiting room." She pushed to her feet.

"Might be fun to watch. How's it been?" He removed his shirt, revealing a cut physique.

"Busy. I've pretty much replaced blood with caffeine in my veins."

He pulled on a clean scrub top and shucked his pants. She averted her gaze until his matching scrub bottoms were put on.

"You've been on for how long?"

"Well over twenty-four. I think closer to thirty-six." She grabbed her bag from her locker and secured it then tossed the bag over her shoulder.

He grabbed his stethoscope and held the door for her. "It will get easier, I promise."

Together they walked to the front desk. She logged out and turned to ask who and where her visitor was when she spied him. Leaning against the far wall, back in a corner, stood none other than Beauregard Jackson.

Manuel stood beside her and handed her a clipboard. She tore her gaze from Beau and looked at what she'd just accepted. An intake from a few hours ago. She'd forgotten to sign.

"Thanks," she said, scrawling her signature along the bottom.

"I actually like you, Mino. Wouldn't want to have to call you to come back after you get out of here in your run for safety and sleep."

She smiled at him. "And I appreciate that more than you can realize. I will see you later. Have a good shift."

Mino edged out from behind the counter and found Beau walking toward her. He stopped when the tips of his cowboy boots hit her Skechers.

"Mino."

Crap on a cracker, his voice was going to give her an orgasm. She'd missed it, missed him. It had been near to six months since their little boot-knocking session in her hotel room.

"Mr. Jackson."

His eyes narrowed briefly before smoothing away to leave a blank expression.

"A moment of your time?"

"While I appreciate you trying to make this sound like I have a choice, seems to me you're telling me I'm giving you a moment of my time. And I don't have any say in the matter one way or the other."

"Are you busy?"

Touch, she just wanted to touch him. Smooth her hands along his torso. Feel the heated skin beneath her palms. Have the thump of his heart moving from him to her. Her fingertips burned with the need to make that small, oh-so-simple connection that meant so much more to her than it ever would to him.

But no, she wasn't busy.

"On my way out. You can walk and talk." She moved past him, determined not to give in to the longing within her.

He fell into step with her and immediately she was warmer. He had a way of doing that to her.

"How are you?"

Mino bit back her irritation. "You could have called to find that out. What do you want to talk to me about?" She stopped outside the hospital, out of the way of any ambulances that would be arriving.

"I want to take you to dinner."

She yawned and shook her head. "Nope. I'm on my way home to bed, I've been here for nearly thirty-six hours and want some sleep."

He glanced around. "Where's your car?"

"I don't have one here. I took the bus."

It was his turn to shake his head. "I'll drive you. Come on."

"Did it ever occur to you I may not want you knowing where I live?" Even as she posed her question she followed him to his vehicle.

"Not like I couldn't find out, Mino."

He held the door to his Charger and she slid over the seat, grateful she didn't have to stay awake on the bus.

The interior shrank when he climbed in and she closed her eyes, just wanting a bit of sleep.

"Where to?"

"You can figure it out, figure it out." She never opened her eyes, just buckled her belt and leaned the seat back a bit.

Mino came to, lying on her couch. The scent of waffles, eggs, bacon and biscuits filled the air. Squinting her eyes, she sat up, gazing about. Beau stood in her small kitchen, back to her, doing something on the stove. She rubbed her eyes and looked once more.

"I'm still here, Mino. No matter how many different times you check."

"Fucker has to have eyes in the back of his head." She got to her feet and stumbled to the kitchen. "What are you doing here?" she asked propping her hand on the doorframe.

"This fucker decided to stay until you woke up so we could talk. And I figured you'd be hungry. Since I know how much you like your breakfast food, I fixed you some."

Oddly touched by that gesture, she was at a loss for words. *Apparently, he either has super hearing or my place is even smaller than I thought.*

Half of her wanted to go back to sleep but the other half was so ready to dive into the food. She was ravenous.

"Give me five minutes and you can eat." He gazed at her briefly.

"Fine."

Mino went and changed out of her clothes, putting on something more comfortable to wear around her apartment. She tugged on her worn Lobo's shirt and workout pants that had the name across her ass. With wolf socks on her feet she made her way out from her bedroom.

Beau dished food up onto plates when she returned. Short of looking at her a few times, he didn't say anything and she was starting to get concerned.

"I'm sorry," she blurted out.

He lifted his gaze, one eyebrow cocked, and shook his head. "For what?"

"Paula."

His expression hardened. "Thank you. It was hard losing a friend."

Yeah, she knew that all too well. He carried the plates to the table then held her chair for her. Beau sat across from her and took a sip of his orange juice.

"Did you go shopping? I don't think I had all this in there."

"Yes." He picked up his fork and ate some of the eggs. "How do you like being a doctor?"

"Not sure. I'm exhausted so I guess good. I'll be happy when I'm out of the ER and can do some stuff in the rural areas."

"Which is what you picked for your specification, right?"

"Right." There was a moment of nothing but two people eating. Then she put down her knife and fork. "What are you doing here?"

"I came to see you."

Okay, she'd not been expecting that. "Why? Fuck buddy have something else to do at this moment?"

"I didn't come down to see her."

"Oh, someone different then." While she struggled to keep her words as uninterested as possible, it wasn't easy. It killed her to think of some other woman having the permission to touch him.

"Yes," he remarked immediately. "Someone different."

"How nice for you."

"One can always hope."

She dropped it. The last thing she cared to do was discuss is romantic interests in someone else. She could be the 'friend' one more time while he waited for her to have some time cleared.

If it was me, I'd be on my back, legs spread, waiting. But hey, this man has that ability to turn me into a whore. What can I say?

"Are you settling in?" he asked, dragging her mind up from the gutter where it quite happily wallowed around in visions of a naked Beau.

"Yes. I just moved to a different place in the same city, not like I moved across the country."

He nodded and put his attention back on the plate. She narrowed her eyes and watched him a bit. He was nervous.

Holy shit. I don't believe I've ever seen him nervous before. Maybe this woman is the one. And it may kill me to say this but I want him happy. I should help him out if I can.

Of course she would. She loved him.

"Beau?"

He met her gaze with his own, his fork still tapping on the plate. There was a bit of hope in his gaze. "Yes?"

"Oh, my God, it's true. You're, like, *nervous* nervous. Are you here to ask her to marry you? Is that why you're acting so unlike you? Are you worried she's going to say no?" She edged closer to him. "I'm sure she's not going to say no. Are you asking her today, is that why you're bumming with me until she's available?" She clapped her hands together, absolutely *refusing* to be sad for herself. "I'm happy for you. Now, what can I do to help?"

Chapter Twelve

Beau stared at her, blinked and continued staring. *What the fuck just happened here? Why does she believe I'm here to marry someone else, or ask them to marry me, and why the hell is she so happy for me to be doing so?*

To state he was confused would be the understatement of the decade. Or the century. Was she seriously acting happy for him believing he was with someone else? Ethan's words came back to him and he realized this was what his cousin had been trying to get him to see and understand.

Mino wouldn't think it was him being there for her because she didn't hold herself in any regard to believe he would want her for more than a fuck. And that was on him. He'd treated her like the other women, a flirty smile and dirty comment, but kept it moving. Even though they'd slept together, she had no reason to trust he would ever want more.

She was good, he'd give her that. There wasn't any sign of hurt in her eyes, just acceptance and happiness for him.

"Have you picked out a ring?"

"No," he said. "Look, I know this is weird, but —"

"Not a problem. I am here to help. I know Anabelle Lee is busy with being pregnant, as is Rally."

"Wait, Rally's pregnant?"

She grinned sheepishly, a blush skimming up her darker cheeks. "Shit. Pretend I didn't say that when Ethan tells you. You know, so you can act surprised."

"When did you find out?"

"She told me two days ago."

Would explain the missed calls from Ethan yesterday. He held up a hand but she waved him off.

"You and I, Beau, we have an odd relationship. I wouldn't call it normal by any means, but you know I'm here for you. So if you need to hang out here until she's free and you can go pop the question, that's fine. If you think she'll be upset about you being here, I understand that too, so you can go. No hard feelings."

"No." He gripped his glass. "No one will tell me who I can and can't be friends with."

"Just don't want to make any waves."

"I've noticed that about you, Mino. Will you ever stand up for what you want? What you feel you deserve?"

"What are you talking about?"

He held her gaze, needing her to see what he was explaining. "I'm talking about you letting what you want slip through your fingers."

A slight hesitation before she shook her head. "I'm not. I have what I want. My degree. The ability to be a doctor and save lives."

"That it?"

She narrowed her eyes. "I guess to you, since it's not out saving the world from one terrorist after another, it's not much. But for me, it's a lot."

God, he was mucking this up. "I didn't mean it like that. Being a doctor is huge and I'm proud you went back to finish up. You've always done great sewing me up."

"Then what are you talking about?"

"Husband? Children? None of this important to you?"

There went that flash of pain on her face, so fleeting he could convince himself it was naught than a figment of his imagination.

"Of course it is. But that doesn't mean it's going to happen."

"What are you looking for in a guy?"

"Why do you care, Beau? Is this a way to keep me from asking about your woman?"

He gave a small smile, praying she'd forgive him for the lie when it all came out. But he needed her to hear him out and if this was what it took, so be it.

"You caught me."

"Honest?"

Well, fuck. He shifted on the seat and gave her an encouraging look to continue.

"I suppose I want him to make me feel safe, be supportive of what I do." She shrugged. "I haven't really thought about it." She pushed to her feet. "Thank you for breakfast, dinner. I'll clean up."

He moved to her living room, getting out of the way—there just wasn't enough space in her tiny kitchen to have them both in there. He called Ethan.

"How goes Operation Get Mino?"

"Fuck you," he said without taking his eyes off the red lettering across her ass.

"I'm sorry, was that Operation Land Mino? Fuck Mino? I forget, what was it now?"

"Operation Kill Cousin."

Ethan laughed. "Okay, fill me in. Then I have some news for you."

He remembered the innocent look on Mino's face when she realized she'd blurted out some news she wasn't supposed to share. Adorably embarrassed.

"She thinks I'm here to ask another woman to marry me."

His cousin choked and it took a bit for him to recover. "I'm sorry, what did you say?"

Beau repeated it and sat on her couch.

"You corrected her, right?"

"No."

Ethan fell silent for a moment before he came back with a loud roar.

"What the hell is wrong with you, man? So you let her continue to think you went all the way out there for another woman? Someone other than Mino? Is that right?"

"She was so happy and excited for me. And she opened up, it took the wall away and…" He shrugged. "I can't tell her now."

"You need to tell her immediately."

"She'll close back up."

"And what the fuck do you think she's going to do when you lose your cool because of something she's wearing or not, and try to kiss her. You're an engaged man and if you try that, or worse, she'll never speak to you again. Hell, she might not anyway because you lied to her."

Beau heard him, truly he did. But his mind was made up. So he grunted at appropriate moments during the dressing down from Ethan and acted surprised when he told him about the upcoming baby, then hung up the phone. Dropping it by his leg, he stretched out and stared over the space to the woman wiping up the counters in the kitchen.

She tucked some loose strands of hair behind her ear as she left the room, moving toward him. Ethan was right on something else—she was going to hate him if he made a move on her.

'Cause the lying will go over so well.

He'd backed himself into a corner. She gave him a smile as she sat. Open and unreserved, a look he hadn't seen since they had first slept together. She'd always been tense and almost uncomfortable. He preferred her like this—this was the Mino he missed, the one he couldn't wait to see.

"Did you reach her?"

"Um, no. But if you have something to do, I can leave."

"You're fine. I don't have a lot of things but I have some games if you'd like to play."

"Beer and games. Sounds like a plan. Grab whichever and I will make a beer run."

"I have beer in the fridge."

"I know, that's the beer run I'm making," he teased with a smile.

Laughing, she went to the hall closet and opened the door. He grabbed two beers and came back to find her still standing in front of it.

"What's the problem?"

He stood behind her and had to curl his hand into a fist so he didn't grasp her around the waist and draw her back against him.

"Not sure which one to bring."

"The one you think you have a chance of winning." He had to force the joking tone past the passion-filled one.

They'd played games many nights late at the office or in one of their homes when it had been him, his cousins and Grams. Mino fit right in with them. Now he understood why — she was the one for him. The woman Grams said would slap him out of left field.

Hell, he'd been with Mino for close to eight years and had gotten so used to her being in his life that being without her was killing him. He'd just been too much of a stupid fucking asshole to see it until it was almost too late for him to do what he had to get his woman.

He reached over her for the Scrabble game. "Let's see what that education taught her."

She elbowed him. "Careful, hillbilly."

He dipped his head and allowed a deep inhalation of her soft scent to embed in his senses. "Hillbilly with two degrees, don't forget that."

"Fuck," she uttered, ducking beneath his arm. "I forgot you're a bit more than hot eye candy."

"Thanks for the vote of confidence."

She didn't look back at him, which was a good thing. He wasn't sure how he was going to handle this, but he had to think up something quick or he was fucked.

He also grabbed Qwirkle from the closet, aware of how much she enjoyed this game as well. At the table, he held them both out to her. "Your choice."

"Start with Qwirkle — it's shorter and that way we're not in the middle of a game when she calls."

It took him a second to remember he was supposed to have a fiancée. Shit, he'd suck out in the field right now were this the situation he had to deal with.

"Scared of my vocabulary?"

"Yes, tractor, lug nut, Kalashnikov, all of those are so hard."

"Don't forget Heckler & Koch. There's also the Dragunov."

She snorted and popped the top off her beer with a quick hit on the table's edge. "Let's do this."

He shook the bag with the tiles for Qwirkle because she wanted that one first and he had zero intention of leaving her this evening.

"Who's going first?" he asked, opening his own beer.

"You're the guest. I'll give you the privilege."

He raked a hand through his hair and got comfortable. "You're going down, Mino."

Her eyes met his and his cock pulsed in his jeans as it took a complete different interpretation of his statement. She put the bottle to her lips and drank. In that moment, his mind drifted back to her on her knees in that tiny hotel bathroom, watching him with her large eyes as he pushed his tattooed cock between her lips and she blew him.

"We'll see."

She had a competitive streak in her that shamed Anabelle Lee's. Right now, Mino's brown gaze had a spark he loved seeing.

Sure, he needed to tell her the truth, but right now, he was going to enjoy the time he got to spend with her. Not anyone else there. No trouble on the horizon. Just him and Mino. How he wanted it to be.

* * * *

Mino wrapped the scarf around her head, tucking it so it would stay in place. Staring at her reflection in the mirror, she sighed. Not a ton of sleep but it would be enough. She tucked a pen in the pocket of her heart scrubs and shoved on her shoes.

Last night and into this morning, she'd had a blast with Beau. That man continued to surprise her. Frightfully brilliant, he'd kicked her ass at Scrabble as if she were in elementary school and he was where he was today.

"Kalashnikov didn't save me at all."

They had chatted and spoken of things she'd not talked about to anyone. Childhood. Fears. Dreams.

He had been amazing at listening.

"Lucky bitch who's getting him."

Part of her had been suspicious he would have tried something, given he knew how weak she was around him, but he had been the perfect gentleman. In that regard. He still cussed and was Beau, but he didn't behave poorly.

She must be some woman for him to have finally turned that corner to act like a man who has the best thing in the world.

It wasn't anything for her to have him crash on her couch because he was Beau. At some point all of his family had stayed with her and she them. She checked her watch and saw she had fifteen minutes to get down to the bus.

Scribbling a quick note for Beau, she turned the knob on her door and peered out. Absolute darkness.

Inching her way up the short hallway, she adjusted to the blackness and kept to the side of the hall, farther from the couch. Not that there was a lot of room for her to go one way or the other. But she didn't want to wake him. He would want to drive her and that wasn't necessary.

In the kitchen, she left the note for him by her coffee maker and picked up her purse from the table by the door. Moving the lock, she then slipped out and hurried down the hall to the elevator.

Earbuds in, she listened to the most recent cozy mystery audiobook she had as she waited for the ABQ RIDE to arrive. With a wave to the driver, she took her typical seat and settled in for the trip to the hospital.

Her day was busy and as she walked out of the building that night, she drew up short. Beau sat in the loading and unloading zone, resting against the hood of his car.

She hurried to him. "You know you can't park here, right?"

"Guess you better hurry and get in then so I don't get in any more trouble." His green eyes sparkled.

"What are you doing here?" she asked, sliding into the car.

"I came to pick you up. Why don't you drive?"

"I don't need to. I'm on a line, so unless I have errands to do after work, there's no point."

He pulled away and she shook her head.

"What?"

"Where's your fiancée?"

He sobered and shook his head. "I haven't asked her yet."

"Either you want to marry her or not, Beau. Quit dragging it out."

"I think she may say no."

"Why would she do that? Surely she loves you and you her."

She flexed her toes in her shoes, not wanting to have this conversation, but he had to go on or she was going to go insane.

"She views me in a certain way and I don't know if she will believe that I've changed."

Mino looked at him. "Changed? How have you changed?"

"No more chasing women kind of changed."

Mino nodded. "Oh, I can see how that would be an issue for a wife."

"Would you?"

She dug in her bag for a bottle of juice and took a sip. "Would I what?"

"Believe me?"

She mulled over her response. "How long has she known you?"

"Let's say as long as you have. And yes, you've seen me with numerous women."

"That's an understatement."

"You know I didn't fuck all of them."

"I'm not expecting any explanation on that, Beau. But honestly, I'd have a hard time believing it. But I'm jaded."

He glanced at her while they waited at a light. "Why are you so jaded?"

A topic she'd avoided last night as well. "That's neither here nor there. I'm sure she's not had to see all the flowers and gifts you've sent to the women, so sure, if I was her I would believe you."

"But since you've seen them?"

"Seen? Beau, again, I sent most of those things. And I think I would have a harder time believing it. But, again, I'm not her so I don't see an issue."

"So, you think I would cheat on a woman I love?"

"Some people consider what we did last night cheating." She put the bottle back as they moved forward again.

"What?"

"It's all about perception. She may view it as you spent the night in another woman's apartment. Nothing happened, but that could be moot as far as she's concerned. I don't know her. I don't want to proclaim to know how she feels about things, but I would assume that she will believe you because she knows what you do. But again, think about it. Even though nothing happened other than two people playing games, to some, we could be the worst people in the world for doing that while you have a fiancée. But if you mean do I think you would fuck another woman once you've pledged yourself. No. I think Mrs. Maybelle raised you better than that."

The silence had her staring at him.

"She does know, right? About what you do? Or have you told her you're like a salesman who has to travel a lot."

He shook his head. "Yeah, she knows what I do."

"Then she has to believe you. Or it's not going to last." He shot her a sharp look and she held up her hands in apology. "I'm sorry, but not every woman will be okay with her husband going off and potentially playing house with another woman if that's what the mission calls for. If she can deal with that, then I would hope she'd believe you when you say she's the only one for you."

"Could you?"

"Could I marry an agent?"

"Yes."

Only one and he is taken. She sighed. "I don't know. Not really something I've thought about."

Liar, her brain yelled.

She ignored its accusatory word. Now wasn't the time for her to tell him she would marry him in a heartbeat. But hey, she had dreams of being with him, where he'd look at her as if she was his whole world and she never had to wonder about him when he was gone. She knew she was his one and only.

"I'm curious."

"Does it matter? I mean, I was on the inside of the business. I know how things operate. I've seen the marriages fall apart from the issues that stemmed from spouses being gone too long, from them getting attached to their fake relationships. It's not something that looks fun to me."

"You're old-fashioned."

"Excuse me?" She angled toward him. "I'm what?"

"Old-fashioned. As in, you like that ideal of one man for one woman. They kiss and the bells ring, sparks fly."

What hit me when we were together. Yes, call me a fucking sap or old-fashioned, it's what I want for my husband.

"Something wrong with that?"

"Not at all. I'm with you on it. That when you meet your one, nothing will keep the two of you from being apart. You move mountains and traverse through hell if you have to in order to stay together."

She gave a low whistle. "Tell her that. It'll work," she replied. *It would for me if some man I loved told me that.*

"I can spin words, Mino, that's not the issue. I know it, so does she. I want her to understand I'm completely head over heels in love with her. One hundred percent in love with her. Nothing will ever change that. No matter what mission I'm on, or what location my duty may take me."

Sure, why not. Add a few more daggers to my meager hope he wanted me. Deflating like a balloon, she struggled to keep the cheer in her voice. "Then you need to tell her these things, Beau. Not me."

"Would you believe it?"

She shrugged. "I'd like to think so."

Why did this have to hurt so much? Life sucked when relegated to the role of friend for the rest of her miserable life. He was her one, she knew that and accepted it, but she also wasn't going to try to keep him from his future. That wasn't how she was built. So she'd swallow her pain, go home and eat a pint of Ben & Jerry's Empower Mint ice cream and cry. Then she'd move on.

Perhaps eat another pint. She loved the mixture of the peppermint ice cream with fudge swirls and brownie pieces in it.

"What do you want to do tonight?" he asked.

"I think you should probably spend time with your girlfriend. Get that popping the question out of the way."

"How would you like to be proposed to?"

"Sorry, Beau." Cripes, how much more did she have to endure? How much more *could* she endure? "You need to do something for her, not that I mentioned for me."

"I know, I just need some ideas."

"Go with what she likes to do or be sappily romantic. I'm sure she'll be happy with however it goes." She unbuckled her belt. "You don't have to park, I can get out here."

He'd barely slowed the car down before she hopped out, trying to make it inside before the tears fell. She closed the door on him calling her name and did the same with the front. Ignoring the elevator, she hoofed it up the stairs.

The tears flowed by the time she closed the door behind her.

"Damn it, damn it, damn it!" She kicked her bag and retreated to the bathroom to shower. "I can't do this anymore. I thought I could. But obviously I can't."

With the water on as hot as she could take it, she thought about where to go after her residency was up. She needed to start over, far away from Beau and the rest of the ones she knew from Theta Corps. Needed to sever ties and move on with her life.

Chapter Thirteen

Furious would be too tame a word to use to describe himself at the moment. Beau longed to punch a hole in the wall beside him. How the fuck she was avoiding him so well was getting to be too much. He was ready to storm the hospital and force her to see him.

All he could get out of her was how busy she was and that she wasn't leaving but catching a few winks on an empty bed in the back. So basically, she wasn't coming out to see him again.

Leaving the emergency room, he touched his ear and called his cousin.

"Good morning, lover boy."

"Stuff it," he growled.

"Oh, so that's how well it is going."

"She's avoiding me." He glanced back to the hospital he'd just left. "Now she's not even going home, just sleeping there."

"She's not going to talk to you until she's ready. Did you clear up the crap about you being engaged?"

"No, and she thinks I am asking someone to marry me, not that I'm already engaged."

"Jesus fucking shit, Beau, are you crazy? Never mind. Obviously you are. I warned you about being able to hurt her. I told you to tell her the truth, to stop with the lies. You've done neither. Now she thinks you're about to be proposing marriage to someone else."

He stopped by his car. "She has to know I love her."

"Give me that phone." Grams' words filtered to him. "Listen to me, Beauregard. You get your ass home right now. I think we need to have a discussion on how you treat women. I don't want to hear any excuses. I expect you home within a day."

The call disconnected.

He didn't want to go home, he wanted to get back in the hospital. But one didn't ignore demands from the family matriarch. Especially on the rare occasion that she cursed. So he listened.

* * * *

Beau made it home early in the morning and had enough time to change before he headed over to Grams' house. He didn't knock, just walked in. She sat at the table, a large bowl of something next to her.

"Get that hat off when you walk into my house."

"Yes, ma'am, Mrs. Maybelle." He removed it and sighed. Hell, he couldn't even get that bit right.

"Sit down, Beau."

He pressed a kiss to her weathered cheek before following her directive. With a peek in the bowl, he saw a bunch of apples.

"Pie?"

"Tarts. And stop calling me Mrs. Maybelle. You are already in trouble so trying to get on my good side by calling me that isn't going to help your case any."

He rose and washed his hands before sitting back and starting in on the peeling, aware it had to be done.

"I have your quilt finished."

"Thank you, Grams."

"You know your father, God rest his soul, had about as much sense as a duck with his bill taped together, still thinking nothing had to change. What the Sam hill are you doing, Beauregard Lee? I raised you better than this."

"I love her, Grams."

She stared at him and deadpanned, "Well, butter my butt and call me a biscuit."

"Sarcasm, Grams." He reached for another apple and began peeling it.

She waved him off. "I've known you've loved her since you first brought her here to the house."

"You couldn't have known. I didn't know."

"That's because you're a man and were too busy thinking with your little head."

"Grams," he begged. It was just plain wrong to discuss his sex life with his grandmother, no matter what she called it.

She rolled her eyes. "Please. I've seen everything you have and cleaned it. My point is, I watched you with her. The other women, you're different in your interactions with them than you are with Shannon. With her, you watch her like she's your world when you think no one else is watching."

It took him a few moments to register that Grams had called Mino by her first name. Something almost no one ever did. *I'm not even sure how the hell she knows that name.* "But you were."

"Of course. You don't think these quilts make themselves, do you? I sit here, I quilt and I observe."

All the truth. "So how do I fix it?"

"I'm not fixing this for you. I like her, a lot. And I want you happy, so figure it out and fix it."

"She is avoiding me."

Grams picked up an apple and threw it at him. Beau caught it purely by reflex. Setting it down, he stared at his grandmother, eyebrows raised in a mixture of shock and disbelief.

"What was the point in that?" he questioned.

"For being an idiot. I love you, Beauregard, but sometimes you make me want to take a switch to you and make you see the light."

"So, what? You want me to kick her door down to make her listen to me? That borders on stalking and potentially threatening someone, Grams."

"Don't be impertinent," she snapped.

"Wouldn't dream of it," he muttered.

The way she glared at him told him she'd heard him just fine and he would end up paying for that smart mouth. He put down the apple and leaned back in his chair, holding the paring knife. With a sigh, he began flipping the knife through his fingers.

"I love her, Grams. It took me a long time to figure this out. Now I've fu—messed up because she thinks I'm wanting to get engaged to a different woman."

"Boy, some days you ain't got the sense God gave a mud puddle. Tell that woman the truth. You know better than to lie to people. I raised you better than that." Grams shook her head.

"It's not that simple."

"It is *exactly* that simple. Now you go and tell her the truth. What happens after then is on you but you owe her that much. Lies are never a good start to a relationship."

Beau nodded. There wasn't any reason in arguing with his grandmother. He wouldn't win. They finished peeling the apples in silence, then he left her with another kiss on the cheek.

* * * *

Both Anabelle Lee and Ethan were at his house when he returned. He dropped his keys on the counter and stared at the both of them. Seated at his kitchen table, eating food.

"Come on in," he said sarcastically.

"We did." Anabelle Lee ate a bit of her sandwich.

Beau couldn't lie, she looked great. Being pregnant added a softness to her she'd never had before and he liked it on her.

"What are you two doing here? And if this is more about Mino, I don't want to hear it. Grams already lectured me on that."

Anabelle Lee popped a pickle chip in her mouth. "I should be pissed you didn't tell me but you told Ethan. Then he reminded me it's a guy thing so I should let it go. Didn't want to. Have this anger thing going on now. Masters says it's not good for the baby but hey, I'm staying as calm as I can."

He shared a glance with her brother. "Is there a point to all this?"

"Yes. We're here to help. What can we do? Get her out here? Go with you to talk to her? What?"

"Nothing."

She huffed and he held up a hand, hoping to ward off the response that would be coming from her.

"I appreciate it, truly I do. But I have to talk to her myself. No more interference. Nothing but the truth and the two of us."

"So you're flying back out to New Mexico today?" Ethan took a drink of his juice, appearing all too satisfied with himself.

Damn expectant fathers.

"Yes. Then I'm going to that hospital and I will have a word with her no matter what."

"Told you, sis."

Beau looked between the siblings. "Told her what?"

"We made a bet on if you'd do it here or go back to her out there. And she now owes me some money."

"Seriously, y'all bet on me?"

They both scrunched up their faces. "You say that like it's never been done before."

Ethan's statement held more truth in it than he cared to think on. Okay, so he couldn't argue with that fact. Rolling his eyes, he walked to his bedroom and pulled out his to-go bag. Dumping out the dirty clothes from last time, he stuffed it with clean ones. Behind him his cousins talked together and he for the most part ignored them.

Ethan was leaning in the doorway when he turned.

"Yes?"

"I have a flight booked for you, sent the deets to your phone. We told Masters not to call you unless absolutely necessary."

"Thanks." He shouldered his bag.

"Good luck."

"Think I'm going to need it?"

"Fuck yes. Especially when she finds out you lied to her about being almost engaged."

Beau sighed. Yeah, he wasn't looking forward to that either.

"I'll see y'all later."

He walked out, aware they would lock up the house when they left, much like he would do to any of their places. Tossing his bag in the truck, he slid behind the wheel.

"I'm fucking nervous." He started the engine, belly in knots. This wasn't right. He didn't do scared, didn't do frightened. He loved the challenge of danger and thrived on the adrenaline that coursed through him during missions. But this one was altogether different.

This was for his future. His woman. His love.

The flight was smooth and it was afternoon when he landed. Making his way out of the Albuquerque airport with his rental, he headed first for her place. *Perhaps she's gone home since I wasn't lurking about for a bit.*

Parking, he shook his head at the sight of her car. It didn't mean a damn thing, because she took the bus more than she drove. Entering the building, he waited at the elevator and stepped in when it arrived.

Moments later he stood before her door and knocked. Tense seconds went by until he heard the locks opening, then the door. And finally, he was face to face before her.

"Beau? What are you doing here?" Her eyes flicked around as if she were waiting for someone to intervene or perhaps find out what the hell was going on. "Is everything okay?"

"No, it's not."

Lord, she made his world right.

Her brow furrowed and she stepped back, waving him in. "What's going on?"

The second the door closed, he wrapped her in his arms and kissed her. His soul calmed as her taste moved through him once more. Having her curves pressed to him helped.

She allowed it for about five seconds, then she smacked his chest and shoved away. "What the hell are you doing?" She took several more steps back from him, none of which took away from how her pupils dilated and her breathing had become erratic. "You're engaged, or you're supposed to be asking her."

"No."

She blinked a few times. "No? No what?"

"I'm not engaged and that woman I told you about was a lie."

Mino's mouth moved but nothing came out for a bit. "A lie?" Eventually the question escaped.

He dropped his bag but stayed near the door. "Yes. And I'm sorry I lied to you but I didn't like you closing me out. And it seemed that once you had latched on to that belief, you were okay with us hanging out together. At least for a little bit."

"You lied."

Beau nodded. "I did, I won't lie to you about it. I was desperate to spend more time with you. And you were so sure we weren't friends."

"We're not."

He pulled back, surprised. "Yes, we are. We've been friends for a long time. Years."

"No, what I've been was useful. And it's always been about you." She pursed her lips and shook her head.

"Mino, that's not true." *Is it?*

"Really? Because you were getting what you wanted, you lied in order to achieve it. The world isn't your op, Beau. People deserve the truth. You don't have to deceive and lie at every turn."

"You were pulling away from me."

"So you lie to keep me close. Do you even know why I was drawing back? You know what? Never mind. It doesn't matter. I need you to leave."

"No. Tell me why."

She wheeled around and walked to her room. The slam of the door spurred him into action. His gut a wreck, he went and pushed into the space she'd just entered. Her bedroom. He took a swift glance to the bed and relived the time he'd spent with her there.

It wasn't enough. He wanted more of those nights. Those days. Just more of it all.

"I'm not leaving, Mino. Call the cops, I'll pull out a fed card. You and I are having this out."

She paused with her hands on the hem of her shirt and glanced at him. "We talk then you leave?"

He didn't want to leave her. Ever. "I'll not stop you from leaving if that's what you want."

"This is my place, Beau. You would be the one to leave. Do we have a deal or not?"

"Deal."

"Turn around."

"What?"

"I'm changing, turn around."

His cock pushed hard in his jeans but he listened, giving her his back. Even as he did that, he watched her in the mirror to his right. Biting his cheek when she yanked her shirt off and put on a purple bra. Then she tugged on a scrub top that had small rainbows all over it.

Mino never once looked back to see if he was doing what he was supposed to, which was *not* look at her. However, he wasn't about to turn down the opportunity to see her beautiful curves.

She kicked off her sweats and pulled on a pair of royal blue scrub bottoms.

Then she spun to him and he moved his eyes from the mirror back to the hallway in front of him.

"You're fine now."

He turned. She sat and tied on some tennis shoes.

"Mino."

"Right. What the hell, I may as well completely embarrass myself. But this is it, Beau. We're done after this. I can't do this anymore. I can't have you showing up at my work wanting to talk to me. None of this showing up at my apartment."

"I want—"

"No. You don't talk now. You wanted me to tell you and I am."

Only this woman was one he would allow to snap at him like this. Well, Mino and Grams. He closed his mouth and waited for her to continue. Worry had set in and he had more than just a tiny bit of concern she was about to break his heart.

Mino dug deep for the confidence and courage she would need to be able to face Beauregard Jackson and tell him her true feelings, then ask him to leave her alone for the rest of her life. Her confidence was on shaky ground and she didn't entirely have the belief in herself that she could pull this off. Not without breaking down into tears or sounding like a babbling idiot. But she had to try, had to or her life would always be this way, not hers but her pining over another she wasn't allowed to have.

She forced herself to look him in the eyes.

"I've loved you for years. Possibly since I first laid eyes on you. When you stepped off the elevator for Masters' office I lost my God-given ability to think clearly. You had this swagger about you I couldn't look away from. This quiet strength I was in awe of."

She began braiding her hair, needing something to keep her hands occupied. He didn't speak, just watched her with that unwavering emerald gaze.

"You actually looked at me when you spoke, not a hello with no eye contact. That meant the world to me, as I was used to being overlooked. Over the years, we learned to laugh and joke with one another. We even fought. All for the good of the country. And you began to use me as your own secretary. Arranging things for your dates, sending gifts, and more."

His expression soured.

"Each time you mentioned your latest conquest it was a dagger to my heart. Not that it mattered, you were that unattainable item for me. The one on the top shelf I'd never be allowed to touch, to have, to enjoy. I wasn't anything like those women. I met my share of them at events and always wanted to tell you how much better you could do. Never did, aside from the jokes."

Holding the end of the braid, she looked around for where she may have left her nearest tie. Beau grabbed one off her dresser and walked to her. Instead of handing it over, he moved behind her on the bed, the mattress dipping with his weight, and tied it for her. It broke her heart to feel his fingers move along the braid before he released it and moved away.

Clearing her throat, she went herself to the door and gestured for him to leave the bedroom. Too much distraction in there with him and her bed in the same place. She needed to remain focused and get this off her chest. Mino waited until he settled in the living room. Rubbing her arms, she breathed deep.

"That was our relationship for years. When Masters and I had our falling out and I left, you were the only one who didn't reach out and see how I was doing. The others did. All except you, the one I wanted to hear from more than anything. And that lack of attempted contact reminded me just how far apart we were. Without me there, forcing myself into your life, you forgot about me."

"That's not true," he interrupted.

"I wish I could believe that. Doesn't matter, not anymore. When you showed up and what happened between us did, that was a mistake. All the times it happened."

His gaze hardened. Apparently, he didn't view it the same way.

She rubbed her hands over the front of her scrubs and went for her windbreaker. Shrugging into it, she observed him. Tense, all the way around. She admired that he wasn't trying to talk over her. Still, she had a bit more to say, then she was leaving. Heading to work.

"Then you tell me this story about being engaged and it quite honestly broke my heart. It reached into my chest cavity and yanked out what was left of my heart and shredded it. We'd just had sex not more than a few days earlier and now you're talking about a different woman you wanted to marry. It was the last straw. I tried to be a friend, but I can't do it anymore. I'm sorry. I have to cut you out of my life because I can't take it. I can't see you married to someone else. I can't see you dating any other women, I just can't. That's such a part of you... I need to distance myself."

Her voice rose and she tried to control her emotions. "I'm not strong enough to do that. I moved across the damn country and you still come and meddle with my heart strings. Now I find out you were lying to me. That is just..."

She shook her head. "Goodbye." Not waiting for him to say anything, she swiped her keys and slipped from the apartment before he could move. She ran to the elevator that was just closing. "Wait for me, please."

Safe inside the car, she watched him in the hall as the doors closed, shutting him out, his expression one she couldn't place. Her heart broke all over again. Betrayal, love lost and just all-around pain.

Goodbye, Beau.

Chapter Fourteen

Mino stood in front of her boss in his office. Donald Gardelli was a good man to work for and she enjoyed his company.

"I know you've been trying to get to a rural area to put your expertise into use, Mino. And I have an opportunity for you if you're interested. It's up near Cuba."

She nodded. "I know the area, I've passed through a few times on my way up to Farmington. Definitely fits the definition of rural in my book. I don't believe they have over a thousand people there."

"I don't think so either, but there is an offer if you'd like to go there and work."

"Absolutely, yes. Thank you for thinking of me."

He pushed an address over to her and she pocketed it after a swift glance to memorize the words written.

"I hate to lose you. You're amazing and going to go far. I am pulling you off rotation and going to say you should head up there and take a look around. I know there is a place to stay that comes with it, but you may not want to stay there. I'll give Gregori a call and let him know you're on your way. If you can be ready to start within the week, he'd appreciate it."

"I'll drive up now. Thank you again, sir."

He shook her hand and walked her to the door. "No, thank you. It's small now but it's growing and there are still going to be ranches around with people who will need help."

With a wave, she hurried off down the hall to her locker. After cleaning it out and saying goodbye to those she would miss, she piled her stuff in her car. Mino got on the road and turned up the music so she wouldn't think about Beau.

Earlier that morning, before Beau stopped by, she'd sent messages to Rally and Anabelle Lee saying how she wished the best for each of them but she needed to break off interactions with them. While she didn't go into much detail, she knew the women would put it together.

Her ride was uneventful and she had newfound excitement in her to keep the sorrow at bay when she parked before the address Donald had given her.

She climbed out of the car and shut the door. The wind whipped around her and she narrowed her eyes against the dirt stinging her skin. It didn't distract her from the raw untamed beauty of the land.

Tonight would be another night of mourning for her past, for the loss of Beau, and a celebration for her moving on. She was stronger than all of these and she would persevere.

* * * *

Beau ignored his phone that was blowing up with texts from Anabelle Lee. He'd read the first one then knew the subsequent ones weren't going to be any nicer or less foulmouthed. He didn't want to deal with her right now.

He swirled the liquor in his glass and readjusted his boots on the foot-rail of the bar. The establishment was pretty much empty. A few of what he figured to be regulars sat and talked low while they drank. Thankfully, they left him alone on the distant end of the bar.

A presence beside him had him turning his head. He cocked an eyebrow and looked at the man who'd sat down without him noticing him even coming in the building.

"The fuck are you doing here?"

The man tugged on the sleeve of his suitcoat. Valentino Cassano sighed and waved for a drink.

"Whiskey, neat." The bartender nodded. "So I see you're in a shitty mood."

"Coming from you, Valentino, that's a laugh."

"I'm totally cheerful now." The man deadpanned his reply, almost making Beau choke.

"Totally?" he asked in a valley-girl tone. "Doubt it but I will say I do see you happier since you got together with Lexi."

Valentine slid money over the bar when his drink was delivered. "So this thing with Mino didn't work out well then." He spun the glass but didn't take a sip.

"Does everyone in Theta know about this?"

"No, only some." He checked his watch. "What are you going to do?"

Draining the whiskey in his glass, Beau then sighed. "Remember when we were in Switzerland and you told me to mind my own fucking business?"

"I do. And I would mind my own business but I actually didn't come here to hold your hand and wipe your ass. I'm here for work. This is merely a fun bonus I get to deal with."

"Don't make me hurt you, Valentino."

"Not worried about that. Are you going to let her go or fight for her?"

"She made it perfectly clear she didn't want anything else to do with me because I am not trustworthy. I lied to her and used her. I'm not good enough for her."

"Of course you're not," Valentino said in a flash. "None of us are good enough for the women who put up with our shit. Answer the question."

He waved for another drink.

"No, I'm not giving up."

"Good to hear. Let's go."

"Go? I'm about to drink some more. Why am I going?"

"Mansfield."

He was off the stool in half a second. "How far and why the fuck didn't you say something sooner?"

"The plane is still refueling. Ethan's on board but I came to get you. Figured you may not try to hit me like you would him."

"Perhaps, but the day isn't over yet." He slapped some bills on the counter. "Let's go." He held up a hand. "Where are we going?"

"India."

* * * *

Beau stood over the man lying on the floor, blood spilling from his leg wound. Hands on his M-4, he waited for the medics to arrive. Beau ignored his own injuries, aware they needed tending to. He had been in hand-to-hand combat, a knife fight and now a gun battle. He'd get looked at later.

Not bad for a day's work. He was bleeding from more than one place, but it didn't matter. They'd succeeded in bringing down Trevor Mansfield and his group. Ethan was part of the ground team that had gone after his right-hand man while he and Valentino had come after Trevor.

The man at his feet coughed and tried to move. Beau stepped on his injury, barely blinking when he cried out.

"You can't do that," he sputtered, his pristine attire filthy and bloody.

Beau spit on the ground. "I could kill you and no one would complain. I may even get a medal for it."

"You can't kill us, we will never be defeated. For every one of us you find, there are ten more waiting in the wings."

"Blah blah blah. Like a hydra. Sure thing. Whatever. We're all real impressed. You know what I don't understand? How you could kill your own brother. Your twin. What kind of sick fucker are you for that?"

"He knew his role. He was there to serve me. To sacrifice for me. And he died with honor."

"There is no honor in strapping your own brother to a bomb." Valentino appeared, looking nothing like the well-dressed man he'd seen before in the bar.

"He's all yours." He patted Valentino on the shoulder and walked away. The choice of what happened to Trevor was his. At least in his mind it was. Beau knew that Masters wanted him alive, but Beau wouldn't be the least bit upset if the fucker didn't make it back.

The medic checked him over and attended his injuries as they waited for the rest of their small team to arrive. The flight back home was quiet and Beau went directly to his house and slept, allowing his broken ribs and bullet wounds to begin their healing process.

* * * *

"What do you mean you're not coming to my shower?"

"Anabelle Lee, I'm tired. Besides, isn't a baby shower for you and your women friends?" Beau winced as he moved too fast and his ribs disagreed. Loudly. "I just got home."

"And you knew about this for a while now. I expect you here. I don't have women friends, I have family and, damn it, I expect my family — that includes you, you ungrateful bastard — to be here for this most joyous occasion! Do *not* make me come for you because I will. No more than ten minutes." She slammed down the phone.

"Yeah, she's handling those mood swings wonderfully."

Joyous occasion his ass.

Beau got out of bed and showered. Dressing slow, he tugged a black Henley over his head then drew on some jeans. Boots on his feet, he took his keys and swiped his hat on the way out of the door. It was nice out, warm, no clouds in the sky with a light breeze.

He drove to her place and found a good number of vehicles there. Most he recognized from work. Touching the bruise on his jaw, he made his way in, removed his hat and hung it on a peg near the door. The noise from inside was loud and boisterous.

Beau forced a smile on his face and headed through to the sliding door to join them. As he neared the kitchen, he drew up and took a sharp breath. Mino stood there, dumping some chips into a bowl.

"Mino," he said a low breath.

Although she'd prepared herself for this moment, the sound of his voice reminded her she wasn't ever going to be prepared for Beau. Biting the inside of her cheek hard enough to draw blood, she pasted a smile on her face and turned toward him.

Holy shit. Her body went on high alert and she wanted to run to him and make sure he was okay. Bruises on his face and, from the way he stood, she had no doubt there were some she couldn't see.

"Beau."

"What are you doing here?"

"Trying not to die."

"I'm sorry, what?" He stepped closer.

She grabbed another bag of chips and popped them open. "Your cousin is a certifiable maniac. She threatened my life if I didn't show up to this. I'd barely gotten off the phone with her when Masters showed up at the door to collect me." It scared the beejeezus out of her how easy it was to fall back into talking with him.

"Yay, she threatened me as well. Can I help you with anything?"

"No, she just said she wanted these chips. Not sure why, there are five other kinds out there, but I'm not about to argue with a crazy woman."

He crossed his arms with a small wince. "And she said you had to do it right now?"

"Yes."

He chuckled.

"What's so funny?" Mino asked.

"She's playing matchmaker."

"With who?" She crumpled up the bags and tossed them.

"Us."

She locked her knees to remain upright. "Pointless on her part."

"Is that so?" He'd moved right beside her.

Mino closed her eyes to try to block him out. It wasn't working. Not even close. "We had this discussion already."

"No, you talked and I listened. I didn't follow you out. I let you run but it doesn't change anything, Mino."

"Sure it does." She prayed, desperate for strength. Loving this man hurt her so much and she wasn't sure she could survive it again.

"No, and you want to know why?"

"Not really. I have to get these out to her before she tries to eat someone."

Mino reached for the bowl only to have him hold it on the countertop. "She doesn't care about the chips. I told you she's matchmaking."

"Let her mess with someone else's life then."

He cupped her face and she couldn't help it, it felt so natural for her to burrow closer to his palm. "Ask me why."

"I'm not playing games with you, Beau."

"I don't want to play games. At least not these kinds with you." He stroked her skin with his thumb. "It doesn't matter because I fell in love."

"No more lies."

"Okay. No more lies."

He turned her to him more and closed the distance, backing her against the counter so she couldn't escape. She gripped the edge so she wouldn't hold on to him.

"I fell in love with a woman who never let me get away with shit. A woman who I would die for in a second. One who lights up a room with her smile. One who always thinks of others before herself, which is why she put aside her own pain to visit a friend this very day."

"So your mystery woman is here?"

"Yes." He lowered his head so it rested on hers. "She's no mystery, though. She knows me better than I know myself."

Her belly erupted in butterflies. "I am not doing this with you."

"We're not doing anything but talking. Remember when I asked you about what you wanted in a man? If you could be with one in this line of work? I wasn't asking for any other reason than I needed to know your answers."

"Doesn't matter," she forced out.

"Respectfully, I disagree, Mino. I asked all those questions because I wanted to know about you. What you thought. How you felt. No one else. *You.*"

Her legs shook and tears burned the backs of her eyes. No, God, not again. She just couldn't. "You lied."

He nodded. "I did and I have no excuse for it other than it allowed me to stay closer to you."

"I hate liars."

He slid some of her hair between his fingers. "I love you."

God help her, she longed to believe him. "You don't get to say that."

He never looked away from her. "Why not? It's the truth. I want what they have, my cousins have, but I want it with you."

"No you don't."

His lips curved up. "You think I don't know what I want, or who? Come with me a moment."

She hesitated.

"I'll bring you right back."

Against her better judgment, she went with him to his truck. He took her to his place and, while she'd been there many times before, this felt different. New, almost.

Mino followed him inside and he took her straight to his office. He opened a desk drawer and pointed. She stepped closer and peered inside. All the cards she'd ever given him. Birthdays, holidays, get well. Every single one.

"And what does this prove?"

"Everything you've given me, Mino, I keep. I don't throw it away. I can't because it was from you." He brought up his calendar. "Your birthday is the only one I have marked on my calendar — I never want to forget it."

Okay, so she'd always gotten something from him. Delivered to her house so no one at work would see. Honestly, she hadn't thought he'd done that, but got a service to.

He drew her back against him. "My job is full of lies, deceit and betrayal. Along with a lot of other things, but you know this."

She did. "Your point?"

"I'm not lying to you about my feelings, Mino. I love you. I want you to wear my ring, carry my name."

"I can't—"

He kissed her. Took her words away and she sank into him, holding on to him in order not to fall down.

"Tell me you no longer love me. Tell me that truthfully and I'll walk away. Tell me there isn't any lingering bit of that love you had for me for so long left within you."

She closed her eyes. "I can't."

"We'll make it work out, Mino." A slight pause. "Please, give me the chance."

Her answer was to kiss him again. She nudged him back until he sat on the edge of his desk. She wrapped her fingers in his hair and deepened the kiss.

"Is that a yes?" he asked between kisses.

"Only if we can stay here for a bit."

His smile warmed her. "As long as you want."

Beau lowered his mouth to kiss her again and she met him halfway, love streaming from her to him and vice versa.

Casanova in Training

Excerpt

Chapter One

Rain ran in rivulets from both his black coat and the brim of his cover. Lieutenant Commander Giovanni Cassano barely moved, even with the loud and angry retorts of gunfire. The noise sounded ominous. Three sets of shots fired by the seven impassive men. He flexed one hand into a fist before relaxing and allowing the smooth glove to straighten.

Through the dreariness, the beginning notes of Taps started to play, weaving in and out of the raindrops with haunting precision. His right hand snapped up in a sharp salute as his shoulders automatically squared even more.

With a deep breath, he fixated on the casket and the two stoic men who had the honour and privilege of folding the flag. Their movements precise and perfected. Each of the thirteen folds corresponded to an important meaning and allowed him to see the wet gloves the men wore. White cotton to his black leather.

First fold was representative of life. He swallowed hard and blinked. Two, three and four took place. The fifth fold, a tribute to the country. Tears burned the corners of his eyes. Six, seven, eight and nine. The tenth fold was a tribute to fathers, for they, too, had given both sons and daughters for the protection of the country since they were first born.

Stiffening his spine, Giovanni clenched his jaw as he watched the remaining three folds to complete the thirteen, so the flag looked like a cocked hat. A reminder of the soldiers who served under George Washington, the sailors and marines who served under Captain John Paul Jones, and all those men and women who followed them in the United States Armed Forces, preserving the rights, privileges and freedoms enjoyed today. As the two men finished folding, the final poignant note faded from the air. And the salutes ended.

He stood ramrod straight. Only his gaze moved as he tracked the presenter who paused before the slender auburn-haired woman clad in black. Michelle Walker. She sat there under a canopy beside her father to accept the flag.

None of the military members there seemed affected by the steady downpour.

"On behalf of a grateful nation," the presenter said, offering the folded flag.

Giovanni saw Michelle hesitate. The man with the flag waited, unmoving, until she finally took it. His hand rose into a salute and, when she gave him a nod, he completed it. The rain increased but Giovanni watched Michelle hold the flag to her chest.

Over the pounding of the rain came the unmistakable sound of fighter jets. He lifted his gaze to see the four planes scream overhead, his heart clenched with a mixture of pain and regrets that he wasn't even close to being ready to face. A lone jet peeled off and his heart did that same thing again. It should have been him up in the one that honoured the fallen man. But no… He had yet to be cleared for flight status.

He ground his jaw and ignored the threatening tears. One by one people filed away, the rain not allowing the mourners any respite. Finally it was him and the two family members. His legs wouldn't cooperate and he had to force them to move him closer.

Stopping at the middle of the closed casket, he took a deep breath, and snapped a salute. "Goodbye, my friend," he murmured before lowering his hand and walking off.

Anger ate at his gut. It was never easy to lose a member of the military. However, when it was a fellow pilot and best friend, it became that much harder.

"Giovanni?" a rattled yet distinctly feminine voice reached him. And halted him.

He swallowed before pivoting around to face her. *Damn it!* For a brief second he was seeing him again. Alive and well. Michael Walker. Sidewinder. Best friend.

She moved closer, the folded flag still clasped tightly to her chest. It hurt looking at her. Mike's twin. A softer, feminine version of Michael, but he was still there in her delicate features.

"Michelle." He hated how gravelled his voice sounded.

Green eyes watched him steadily. "You were going to leave without a word?"

He put his gaze on their…her father. Martin Walker showed his age. He seemed so tired and worn out. However, in his eyes, there was anger. The siblings had taken after their mother. Giovanni had always teased Mike about being so pretty. Now his body had been so badly burnt and mangled it had had to be a closed-casket ceremony.

"No," he managed to say as he glanced from father to daughter. "I was going to wait by the car. Allow you final moments."

Martin shook his hand briefly then nudged Michelle. She lifted one gloved hand to wipe the tears from her eyes. "Take this." She held the flag out to him.

His heart seized as he glanced at the flag. *Stars uppermost to remind us of our nation's motto.*

"No. I can't. That is for you."

Her smile was shaky at best. "Mike would want you to have it."

Giovanni glanced to Martin, ready to plead his case, only to pause. The look Martin bore told him the flag wouldn't be going back with them. Martin was in a rage from having just buried his only son. He focused on Michelle and saw the opposite. She loathed to give it up and was only doing so for her father.

Almost as if he hovered outside his body, he saw himself reaching for the flag. Michelle relinquished it to him but didn't step back. Instead, she lifted his hand, pressed the flag against his chest, and hugged him.

"Keep him safe," she whispered in his ear.

More of those damn tears threatened. "When you're ready to take it…" He trailed off.

"Thank you, Giovanni."

"Michelle!" Martin barked.

She flinched at the tone but squeezed him one more time. A quick peck on the lips and she was gone. They were gone. Moreover, he stood in the raining cemetery, holding the flag given for the loss of his best friend's life. The thunder rolled, ominous, and the rain picked up even more.

He needed a drink. Badly. And, after he returned to his hotel room and changed from his uniform, he set off to do just that.

* * * *

The bar was crowded and noisy. Just what he
wanted—a place to become invisible. He claimed a
corner booth and sat there, bottle of Jack on the table
beside him. He poured a drink for his fallen friend and
drank it.

"Here's to you, Sidewinder."

Then he did his best to forget the pain inside him. He
knew what Mike would have said. "Find a woman and
enjoy life. Don't cry for me."

Easier to think than to do. With dispassionate eyes, he
watched the activity around him. Many women
sauntered up to him, only to leave again when he
ignored them.

He poured another drink, craving the blur it made of
his memory. He paused with his glass halfway to his
lips. An unfamiliar tingle skated along the back of his
neck. Glancing around the establishment, he found
himself focusing on a woman he didn't recognise or
recall entering. She sat with another but he couldn't
look away from her.

She had skin that reminded him of hot chocolate, with
some whipped cream blended in. Lickable. Black hair
drawn up and away from her face in a ponytail, it fell
down to almost her shoulder blades. A low, purely
animalistic reaction hit him square in the gut. His cock
sprang to attention and he was halfway out of the booth
before he realised it.

He sat back down, continuing to stare unabashedly at
her. He could see she wore an ice blue crossover top.
All he longed to do was trail the straps with his tongue
and see where they would lead. Discover her taste, her
smell.

Her head fell back and her laughter—he assumed it was laughter by the smile on her and the other woman's faces—seemed to add to the glow about her. He scowled when two rather large men blocked his view.

Draining his drink, he pushed to his feet then headed over there. It made absolutely no sense, especially for not having even been introduced to her, how possessive he felt towards this mystery woman. He came up around them and immediately his gaze honed in on her.

Yes, definitely lickable. And biteable.

She had full lips he wanted to kiss, a small, cute nose, and large eyes that were framed by thick, curved lashes. A punch to his solar plexus had him sucking for air when she pinned her gaze on him. Those eyes were killers, multi-hued like a tortoiseshell, and he felt himself willingly falling in.

He glanced at the other two men, moved his gaze on to the second woman before settling once more on his woman. "Dance with me." It wasn't a question or a request, but that was his way.

She stared at him, her unique eyes assessing, and he fought the urge to shift when he believed she'd seen past the outer shell. A slight grin lifted the corners of her lush mouth.

"Sure." Her voice fell smooth, thick, and rich like honey.

She slid from the booth and he held his ground so she would have to brush against him. A plan that didn't work as he'd intended. His cock was ready to punch free at the tantalising sweep of her full breasts across his chest.

"Let's go," she said with a smile that made him think about thrusting his shaft in and out of her mouth.

Gesturing for her to lead the way, he followed the seductive sway of her hips, which were draped in a tight, white leather skirt. He groaned and dragged his gaze down and over her long, lean legs and her fuck-me heels the same colour as her shirt.

Fuck!

He almost lost it right then and there. So he lengthened his stride to catch up to her. With those sexy heels, she would fit just right against him. He guessed her height without heels to be about five-seven.

She tossed her head and rotated back to him. Her gaze took another trip along his body and he bit back his responding groan. The music changed to a slow, sultry ballad. Her eyes showed her hesitation and he reached out to draw her close before she left him standing there.

A flirtatious smile lifted her lips as she willingly came closer to him. Her bare arms slipped around his neck and he took a shuddering breath when she pressed tight against him. Ignoring the fire in his blood, he placed his hands at her waist, fingers grazing the small of her back.

"What's with guys and issuing demands? You could have asked me to dance, you know."

He slid his hands around to cup her ass, bringing her flush to his blatant erection. "You could have said no."

"I get the feeling that isn't a word you hear very often."

It was true. His call sign wasn't Casanova without good reason. "Not too much."

Her fingers stroked along the back of his neck. He felt on fire, both inside and out. Each step took them closer to the edge of the dance floor. By the time the song ended, the two of them were in a darker hallway.

He lowered his head, giving her half a second to stop him. She didn't. Her mouth met his. She played the aggressor, sliding her tongue in and around his. Lust blazed to life in him and he ground into her, making his desire very clear. She moaned, a sexy sound—it came from the back of her throat and moved through him like electricity.

His grip on her grew possessive as he took control of the kiss. She tasted like mint. Not peppermint or spearmint. Raw mint. Pure mint. It was addictive as hell and he couldn't get enough. The feel of her against him, the taste of her—together they lessened the pain that had consumed him since the accident.

He tore his mouth from hers and nibbled his way down her neck. Her gasp of pleasure coinciding with how she tilted her head to give him better access spurred him on. It didn't matter that they were in a busy bar hallway. All that mattered was her. And sinking his hard length fully within her molten heat.

His hands began moving beneath her short skirt, seeking his prize. She pushed on him and he drew back to glance down at her. Flushed. Passionate. Delectable.

"Hold on there, handsome. I'm not into exhibitionism."

He gazed to his right and saw two men loitering there. Voyeuristic pleasure on their faces. "Go!" he said in a growl so low the word was hard to decipher.

The meaning not. They left after only a few more leers at the woman in his arms. Again alone, he placed his gaze back on her. He held her stare before slanting his mouth back over hers.

"We need to stop," she said, a bit breathlessly, when he broke the kiss.

"Why?"

She took some deep breaths. "I came for a dance with you. Not to get fucked against a wall." She gave him a small grin. "Besides, I'm the DD and I have to get them home."

Fury licked at his veins. "Don't go with them. Those guys aren't right for you." What'd she need two of them for? He was more than enough for her.

She tipped her head back and laughed. A vibrant sound that made his knees shake.

"That's cute, really. You think you know what's best for me based on one dance and having your tongue down my throat." It wasn't a question. "Those two are like brothers to me, not that it's any of your biz. Now I have to go. Early flight."

She gently removed his touch from her then stepped around him. Unwilling to let her go, he captured her wrist and tugged. "Come with me."

"You're good," she said with a small sigh. "Too good. That's another thing I don't do. You've got to me enough to get this far."

She captured her lower lip in her teeth before moving nearer. With her free hand, she cupped the back of his head and pulled him close. Her eyes darkened and she kissed him. Her nails scored the back of his head as her tongue invaded. He went from controlled to locked and loaded in a flash.

The kiss ended and she pulled back. "Goodbye."

Then she walked away. Her friends met her and he moved towards them to hear her voice. Her laughter. She expertly herded her group to the door where she paused and glanced back at him. Her eyes flared with heat and it took every last ounce of his control to remain where he was. In a flash of blue and white, she was gone and his world got considerably darker.

"I'm available."

At the statement, he looked to see a woman dressed in too-tight clothing. "Of that I have no doubt."

He strode off, ignoring her gasp of outrage. Barely slowing, he grabbed his jacket and made his way to the door. The night hadn't gone exactly according to plan. With a snarl of frustration, he waved for a taxi. Slumping in the back seat, he gave the hotel before closing his eyes and using his memory to recreate the vixen from tonight.

He half stumbled from the taxi to his room, only to fall face first across his king-sized bed. Yep. He was close to wasted. Real close. Granted, touching his mystery woman had made the drinks' effects slip away. All his focus had been on her, her minty flavour and that skin, that delectable, tempting, hot-chocolate skin.

All he'd wanted to do was bite, lick, and suck. Christ, even now — just thinking of her — his cock stiffened in his pants. He wanted her bad. Yes, he'd loved women before, but this was different. This woman got to him on a molecular level.

"Fuck it!" he uttered, flopping on to his back. Eyes closed he tried to forget he'd just buried his best friend.

He slept through all of the next day and was back at the bar the following night. Sat in the same booth and watched the door. He only nursed his drink this time. Hours passed, and he was ready to get up and leave when someone slid in across from him. He snapped his head over to growl, only to find himself staring into sparkling tortoiseshell eyes.

It took him a few moments to remember to breathe. She put his visual recollection of her to shame. Unlike last night, her hair fell loose around her face. Her large eyes peered at him unblinkingly. *How did she get here without me knowing?*

She reached out and took his drink from him, moving it to the side. He reacted swiftly, capturing her hand in his. Hers was almost delicate, but he could feel both strength and calluses. He threaded their fingers, pleased to be touching her again, and returned his gaze to her face.

"Thought you had an early flight." He stroked the inside of her wrist with his thumb.

"I missed it."

"Babysitting tonight?"

"Nope."

He swallowed. "Come with me."

Her response was to get to her feet and tug him up. He went willingly and drew her in close. Damn but he wanted to kiss her. Her confusion when he didn't was obvious.

"I kiss you now, sweets, and we will be fucking right here on this table." He watched heat flare in her eyes, making them almost molten gold. "Let's go."

He slid his arm around her waist and headed for the door. He moved the tips of his fingers in small circles on her hip. Outside he waved for a cab then looked at her.

She wore another amazing outfit. A tight ribbed coral tank top and another short leather skirt, black this time. More fuck-me heels, the colour of which matched her shirt.

"Why'd you come back?" he asked as the cab took them to his hotel.

"I don't know. I tried to get on the plane but I couldn't."

He leaned close and nuzzled the side of her neck. She smelt as delicious as she had yesterday. He licked along her pulse and his cock throbbed at her answering moan.

"You okay with this?" He had to be sure.

She moved her head to the side, giving him better access. "Yes," she said on a breathy sigh.

He shifted and placed his hand on her thigh, stroking just above her knee on the inside. He kissed her. Sucked on her tongue and searched for all the corners he could find. She leaned into him, one hand settling on his chest. Her response was explosive and he wanted to be away from public eyes.

The cab stopped and he barely looked at the man before tossing him some bills to cover the fare. Her hand in his, he led the way to his room. He was on her the second the door closed behind them.

Control gone, he dominated her mouth as he gripped her ass and pulled her flush to his rampant erection, ensuring she felt it. Her fingers threaded in his hair, pulling lightly, and he growled, a warning, or a promise, he wasn't sure.

"Bed," he rasped, tearing his mouth from hers. God, he was burning up. From the inside out.

"No. Here. Now."

He fished a condom out of his pocket, freed himself, then sheathed his stiff cock. Pushing up her skirt, he found a fire-engine-red lace thong. "Shit, you're killing me here."

He yanked on it, relishing how it snapped beneath his tug. There was no foreplay and no gentle words of love. He gripped the base of his cock and moved it along her wet slit then slammed home hard. Her scream of pleasure raced up his spine.

Fuck me! He began to move within her hot, tight pussy as the velvet walls held him.

Fuck me!

Jaydee Amos moaned again and again, as the man pinning her against the wall drilled his cock into her over and over. He stretched her, filled her, and blew her mind. It was rough, and not at all sweet or tender. It was perfect.

His mouth latched on to her neck as he thrust into her. She scraped her nails along the back of his neck and shoulder. Lifting a leg, she hooked it around his waist. He grunted, palmed a breast, and moved faster. She came hard when he tweaked her nipple and grazed his teeth along her neck. He erupted soon after that, his powerful body shuddering before seeming to sink into her.

He drew back and she smiled at him, a languid smile. A well-pleasured smile. His tanned skin was covered in sweat. He had hazel eyes that burned with hunger. One hand brushed some of her sweaty hair back.

"Bed now," he demanded, whipping off his shirt.

Her mouth went dry at the sight of his chiselled torso. He was all ridges and rippling muscles. She reached out to touch him, felt the sweat and dragged her fingers over one pectoral. Inside her, his cock hardened.

When he withdrew, she bit back a whimper of disappointment. One that changed to a moan of approval as he shucked the rest of his clothes. Not an ounce of fat on him. His cock, again hard, stood out proudly from a nest of black hair. It was bare and the evidence of his cum was smeared along the head. He'd disposed of the condom. She stretched out to touch him, only to stop at his gravelled command.

"Undress."

She removed her shirt and followed with her bra. His eyes darkened and she moved to her skirt. His cock bobbed and it sidetracked her for a moment.

"Leave the shoes," he said, dragging a finger around one puckered nipple.

So she did.

He laid her back on the bed and settled himself between her legs. She stared at him, lost in the intensity of his eyes. His fingers skimmed over her pussy and she widened her legs in silent invitation. He ripped open another condom and covered himself. She didn't even recall him grabbing more foil packets. Then he slid the broad head of his shaft into her and nothing else mattered. Over and over again, he escorted her to the pinnacle of pleasure only to back off and start over. The first time had taken the edge off his need and now he seemed content to go slow. She burned all over as he flexed in her with nice, easy strokes.

"Harder." She worked her internal muscles.

He shuddered. "Slow and gentle."

Her protest was stopped when he drew a nipple into the warmth of his mouth.

"Ahh!" she cried, arching into him. "Oh…yes… sweet…" She continued to babble as he thrust in tandem with the sucks on her breast. So many sensations bombarded her.

His rumble vibrated against her nipple as he powered deep and she exploded around him. She gripped him as he released the control and pistoned his hips into her. Over and over. Unrelenting. Like a machine. Willingly, she met each thrust, hungry for more, her heels grinding into his ass. He came with a roar and collapsed on her. The room smelt of sex and sweat.

Exhausted, she barely moved when he withdrew and left the bed. She cracked her eyes open when his touch was on her feet. *How sweet, he's removing my shoes.*

Boneless, Jaydee sank against him after he turned off the light, climbed back into bed, and covered them with the blankets. Thoughts of leaving were the furthest thing from her mind as he draped a corded, muscular arm over her waist and tucked her in close. She fell asleep with his deep breathing in her ear and his scent in her nose. There was also the warmth and security of his touch.

* * * *

She woke and lay still as her mind worked out where she was. This wasn't her bed. Strong arms curled around her body, keeping her near…and warm. A head nestled into her breasts, stubble abrading her skin with each breath she took. She sought the clock and sighed. *Time to get going.*

How to untangle herself? She shifted to the side only to freeze when warm lips settled over one nipple, drawing tight. Desire unfurled within her and she moaned, arching, before she realised it.

A moan that turned to a cry of pleasure as he sank two fingers into her pussy. Her last coherent thought was, *I can leave later.* He brought her to another explosive orgasm, draining what little energy she actually had left. So, again, sated and fatigued, she drifted back off to sleep.

Twice more she woke and attempted to sneak away. Twice more he fucked her back into exhaustion. The third time she opened her eyes and just lay there. She was so sore. In a good way, but so sore.

"Close your eyes," a deep voice said.

Turning her head, she found him staring down at her. Him. *I don't even know his name.* His hazel eyes still smouldered and, despite everything, she felt herself respond.

"I need to get up."

"I am up," he said with a languid wink. One large hand skimmed over her belly before settling with familiarity on her pussy. He used a lone finger to stroke her and she bit back her purr of contentment as she widened her legs.

"Good girl." In and out he moved the single digit. "I think I could get used to this in the morning," he muttered in her ear as he slid inside her willing body with one smooth thrust.

Me too.

Accepting she'd not be leaving the bed anytime soon, she gave herself over to her stranger's masterful touch. They spent all day in bed. One time when she woke, he'd brought some food to the room. After which they went back to bed. She didn't understand, she was supposed to get him out of her blood yet the longer she was there it felt like he was deeper in it.

She urged her aching body out of bed and dressed while he was in the shower. Sure, it was the coward's way out but she knew all it would take was one touch from him and leaving would fall by the wayside. One ear tuned to the shower, she shoved her feet into her shoes and made a call.

With one last, longing look to the closed bathroom door, she bit her lower lip and slipped from the hotel room, totally not understanding why leaving this man—whose name she still didn't know—was so difficult. Forcing herself to leave, she closed the door behind her. She took a deep breath and strode from the hotel, clad in her club wear with her head held high. Not much later, a black Mitsubishi Spyder roared up to the entrance and she climbed in.

"Almost a day," the woman behind the wheel said.

"Stuff it, Lexy." There was no malice in her tone.

"Same guy as the previous night?"

She hung her head. "I couldn't help it. There is... was...something about him."

Lexy laughed. "I'm sure. I saw the two of you in the hall at the bar." A sideways glance. "Are you hungry? Bet y'all didn't come up for air much."

She ground her teeth at Lexy's over-syrupy Southern drawl. "Bitch."

Another laugh as Lexy tore around a truck going too slow in her estimation. "You know it. Besides, I would assume you'd want to go change and hide that big-ass hickey on your neck. I bet you have them other places, too. Don't you? Thighs? Ass?"

"Drive, you foul-mouthed bitch."

Jaydee leaned her head against the window and closed her eyes. Even now, she could feel the caress of his callused hands on her skin. Moisture began to flow and she shifted on the seat.

Lexy whipped into her drive and pulled into the garage. "Come on, you go shower and change while I make you some food."

It was already dark, had been when she left the hotel, and Jaydee's stomach growled. "Thanks, Lexy." She trudged, sore and tired, into the house then to the guest room. After showering and dressing in something a bit more conservative — a bit more her — Jaydee made more flight plans. She had to get to her destination — staying longer had cut into her time of learning the area.

After a filling meal, Lexy drove her to the airport and dropped her off. They shared a hug.

"I want to know about this guy."

"I told you everything over dinner, Lexy." She grabbed her bags and headed for the door. "I'll call you when I land. Thanks for everything."

"Name!" Lexy yelled. "What's his name?"

Glancing back, she shrugged and placed her bags down. "I don't know, we never exchanged them."

Lexy's grey eyes grew wide as an ear-to-ear grin split her face. With a fist pump, she gave a wolf whistle. "I always knew you had it in you. Love you!"

Jaydee rolled her eyes and ignored the stares. With a wave over her shoulder, she grabbed her luggage again and continued. Once on board the plane, she settled in her seat and sobered. There was a lot of work to be done at her new duty station. Best to be met with a clear head. She covered up with a blanket and closed her eyes, settling in for the flight. Jaydee fell asleep even before they reached cruising altitude.

* * * *

Two weeks later, Jaydee's boots made very little noise as she headed to the briefing room. Her belly was full of knots, although she ensured none of her distress or unease displayed on her face. It was always difficult coming in to a new squadron. Even a test pilot one. And even more so when she was replacing a fallen pilot and friend.

Voices, loud and male, drifted out into the hall and to her ears.

"Who's taking his place?" A slight pause. "I mean who's filling his spot? Sorry, Casanova, I know no one can take Sidewinder's place."

Casanova? Well, guess it isn't hard to figure out what he's done to get that nickname.

The response was too low for her to make out. Then another man spoke. "Lieutenant Commander Jaydee Amos, call sign Dusti."

She paused right before entering. They were talking about her and she bet anything they were assuming her first name was initials. It normally happened. The next speaker's voice made her pause it was filled with so much anger. "Jaydee, never heard of him."

She was right—they assumed she was a male.

"Comes highly praised. Apparently some sort of hotshot pilot."

"We'll see." The angry one spoke again.

Jaydee forced her legs to carry her into the room. Silence descended as numerous gazes fell upon her. A low whistle filled the air and several men eyed her up and down as if she was their next meal.

"You seen the new chick, Casanova?" a blond asked.

"Who are you?" a different blond questioned.

She opened her mouth to answer only to see another man step into her line of sight. Her body reacted violently and expediently. Staring back at her was tall, dark and handsome from her wild and impetuous twenty-four-hour dalliance.

Male laughter erupted. "Looks like she's already smitten with Casanova."

He's Casanova? Hell, he's a pilot? And why is he here? She rallied and drew on the ice that flowed through her veins. Unbidden, her gaze drifted back to Casanova. His beautiful hazel eyes had narrowed suspiciously as he stared at her. She'd been doubted because of her gender before, it wasn't anything new.

"Who are you?" The question was repeated.

She answered simply, "I'm Lieutenant Commander Amos."

You could have heard a pin drop. Casanova's features hardened.

"Hell no!" he snapped, fire blazing from his eyes. "You're the pilot? Jaydee?"

She couldn't believe this was the same man who'd loved her so thoroughly and completely that night two weeks ago. A gaze that had smouldered and stared at her with relentless hunger were now furious.

"That's me. Many people assume I'm a man from my name." She shrugged. "I'm not."

"You're a girl."

Derision dripped from his words. He prowled towards her, looking all kinds of hot in his flight suit. Around them, the room fell silent. She held his stare, her expression blank. He stalked around her, teasing her senses. Again, face to face, he scowled at her.

"Have you even flown a B-2?"

All remaining gentle feelings towards him about their shared night vanished in a puff of smoke. "Obviously, or they wouldn't have sent me. Don't try to measure your dick to mine, Commander. You're sure to come up short."

Laughter erupted around them yet she ignored everything but the man going toe to toe with her. He crossed his arms, his glower deepening. It took a bit of time for her to ignore the power she knew rippled beneath the flight suit.

"Can it, Cassano!" a new voice intruded. "Leave her alone. Listen up, everyone. We've been a man down with the loss of Walker, and Amos here is filling in. Until we get a permanent pilot assigned."

"Better not be too long," Casanova muttered beside her.

"Listen up, Cassano," the CO demanded. "Nothing fancy today. We'll brief in the air. Make sure you introduce yourself to Amos." He slammed his book shut and left. Leaving her to fend for herself.

A blond man—the one who'd previously called her 'chick'—approached her, his blue eyes sharp and assessing. "I'm Keel. You're my pilot."

She nodded, understanding that, if they were called up, he'd be the mission commander. "Dusti." Keel didn't offer his hand, just sized her up. There were two other women there in the room, but they didn't look any happier to see her then the men did.

"Meet you at the bird."

She nodded and watched the others leave. Falling in behind a cocky lieutenant, she reached the door a second before it slammed in her face. Tall, dark and handsome leaned against her exit from the room. Arms crossed. The pure sexuality he oozed made her waver a second. The anger in his eyes cooled her ardour.

"You're in my way, Commander," she said without intonation.

"You ran from me while I was in the shower."

She blinked. His words shocked her, for she hadn't thought he would have mentioned it. "You're still in my way."

"Women shouldn't be flying in combat."

"This is a training facility and you need to move."

"We need to talk," he rumbled.

"No, we do not. Now get out of my way."

With a mocking smile and an exaggerated bow, he opened the door for her, only to fall in behind her. All eyes were on them as they strolled from the building, now side by side. They peeled off and she surreptitiously stole a final glance as he sauntered to his plane. He was a man who was the epitome of a fighter pilot. An unmistakable swagger and an ego the size of the sun.

Striding up to her jet, she stared at the impressive B-2. The bombers were lethal, dangerous and, to her, absolutely beautiful. She loved flying them. The excitement built, spreading throughout her as she talked to the mechanic for her new bird. His name was Tory Sedin, a Petty Officer First Class.

About the Author

Aliyah Burke is an avid reader and is never far from pen and paper (or the computer). She is happily married to a career military man. They are owned by six Borzoi. She spends her days at the day job, writing, and working with her dogs.

Aliyah loves to hear from readers. You can find her contact information, website details and author profile page at http://www.totallybound.com.